almost identical

....

DOUBLE-CROSSED

almost identical

....

DOUBLE-CROSSED

by Lin Oliver

Grosset & Dunlap
An Imprint of Penguin Group (USA) Inc.

GROSSET & DUNLAP
Published by the Penguin Group
Penguin Group (USA) Inc., 375 Hudson Street, New York, New York 10014, USA
Penguin Group (Canada), 90 Eglinton Avenue East, Suite 700,
Toronto, Ontario M4P 2Y3, Canada (a division of Pearson Penguin Canada Inc.)
Penguin Books Ltd, 80 Strand, London WC2R 0RL, England
Penguin Ireland, 25 St Stephen's Green, Dublin 2, Ireland
(a division of Penguin Books Ltd)
Penguin Group (Australia), 707 Collins Street, Melbourne, Victoria 3008, Australia
(a division of Pearson Australia Group Pty Ltd)
Penguin Books India Pvt Ltd, 11 Community Centre,
Panchsheel Park, New Delhi–110 017, India
Penguin Group (NZ), 67 Apollo Drive, Rosedale, Auckland 0632, New Zealand
(a division of Pearson New Zealand Ltd)
Penguin Books (South Africa), Rosebank Office Park, 181 Jan Smuts Avenue,
Parktown North 2193, South Africa
Penguin China, B7 Jiaming Center, 27 East Third Ring Road North,
Chaoyang District, Beijing 100020, China

Penguin Books Ltd, Registered Offices: 80 Strand, London WC2R 0RL, England

Cover illustration by Mallory Grigg

Text copyright © 2013 by Lin Oliver. All rights reserved. Published by Grosset & Dunlap,
a division of Penguin Young Readers Group, 345 Hudson Street, New York, New York 10014.
GROSSET & DUNLAP is a trademark of Penguin Group (USA) Inc. Printed in the U.S.A.

Library of Congress Cataloging-in-Publication Data is available.

ISBN 978-0-448-45193-0 (pbk)   10 9 8 7 6 5 4 3 2 1
ISBN 978-0-448-46161-8 (hc)   10 9 8 7 6 5 4 3 2 1

ALWAYS LEARNING   PEARSON

*For Amanda Bickman,
my wonderful niece and great advisor—LO*

The New Boys

....

Chapter 1

"The new boys are here!" my twin sister, Charlie, shouted as I jogged across the beach to the lounge chair where she was sprawled out sipping a strawberry smoothie.

Before you get the wrong impression of me, let me tell you right off that I am not a major jogger. In fact, the only thing I hate more than jogging is running. And the only thing I hate more than running is running fast. I think you get the point. But my dad has me on his super-duper "shape up, slim down" program for our next tennis tournament. (Oh, did I mention that Charlie and I are ranked doubles tennis players? Well, we are.) Anyway, if I take a daily run, my dad, who is also our coach, lets me have fries on the weekend. I'd say that's worth a twenty-minute jog.

"What boys are you talking about?" I asked, grabbing the smoothie from Charlie's hand and taking a giant slurp. "Ouch. Brain freeze."

"Press your thumb against the roof of your mouth," Charlie suggested.

"Why? So I can look stupid?"

"Because it warms your mouth, and gets rid of the brain freeze. Honestly, Sammie, everyone knows that."

I shrugged but did it anyway, and after about ten seconds, the brain freeze went away. Unfortunately, what didn't go away was our older brother, Ryan, who was hanging out on the deck, juggling a volleyball in his hands. The minute I stuck my thumb in my mouth, he dropped the ball, reached into his pocket, pulled out his phone, and snapped a picture of me.

"Nice thumb-sucking," he commented, checking out my image on the screen. "Oh, and just a little heads-up, Sammie. That's not a real popular look in the seventh grade."

"Delete it, Ry," I ordered.

"I was thinking that the new boys might enjoy seeing this picture. Along with your other new pals at Beachside Middle School. What's it worth to you for me to delete it?"

I lunged for his phone, but he held it up high above his head where I couldn't reach it. Ryan has always been tall, but he's in the middle of his fourteen-year-old growth spurt, and now he's such a beanpole that I can't jump high enough to knock anything out of his immense hands. Charlie can because she weighs less than me, so when she jumps, she goes higher. That's one advantage of being the thinner twin.

Oh yeah, there's also one other minor advantage— all the boys think she's hot. There is that little detail.

Anyway, the higher Ryan held his phone, the more I jumped, mostly just to harass him. Eventually it worked.

"Okay, okay, if you get out of my face, I'll delete it," he said. "On one condition. You tell me who these new boys are. Spill it. Could our little Sam-I-Am be having a hot romance?"

"I don't know what you're talking about, Ryan. I don't know any *new* boys. I barely know any *old* boys."

"Well, I know who they are," Charlie said. "Their names are Eddie and Oscar."

I just stared at Charlie blankly. None of this was ringing a bell.

"Alicia called when you were jogging," Charlie said. "Or what you laughingly call jogging because it looks more like creeping. Anyway, she said to tell you her cousins Eddie and Oscar have arrived and she wants to bring them over to say hi."

Ding, ding, ding. A bell rang inside my head. I remembered that when I walked Alicia to her bus stop after school last week, she had mentioned that her twin cousins were coming to visit Los Angeles from El Salvador. She never mentioned their names, though, and I never gave it a second thought.

"Listen, Sammie," Charlie said, and from her tone of voice I knew she was annoyed. "I'm having a little get-together here at the club, and it's just for my friends."

"Don't worry, I don't plan on busting up your party, if that's what you mean," I told her.

"But what about Alicia and her cousins?" Charlie asked, trying to be delicate. "Not to be rude or anything, but—"

"First of all, Charlie," I interrupted, "Alicia is coming over to see me. As in *me*, not *you*. And about her cousins—let's just assume that two teenage guys haven't traveled all the way from El Salvador to hang around and discuss lip gloss with you and your friends."

"We discuss other things than lip gloss," Charlie shot back, pretending to be hurt. "We're not totally shallow."

"Yeah." Ryan laughed. "Like just yesterday I heard them discussing spray tans. Nothing shallow about that."

Charlie and I both rolled our eyes at Ryan. She and I have our differences, but we are united in our reactions to Ryan's so-called humorous comments about our lives. He never stops teasing us about everything—how we both dot our *i*'s with a circle, how we both bite our nails, and how neither of us can boogie board without wearing a nose clip.

I know you're thinking that the nose clip thing

probably doesn't come up very often, but actually, it does. We live at the beach, and that involves a lot of boogie boarding and nose clip wearing.

Our family recently moved into the Sporty Forty Beach Club, a white wooden cottage with blue shutters that sits right on the sands of Santa Monica beach, between Los Angeles and Malibu. We're not rich like the forty families who are the club's members—in fact we're the opposite of rich. We live in the caretaker's bungalow because my dad is working as the tennis coach at the club while my mom is away at cooking school.

Ever since we moved in a couple months ago, Charlie has become really close friends with all the members' kids, who call themselves the Sporty Forty 2s, as in second generation. My new best friend, Alicia Bermudez, is the daughter of Candido and Esperanza, who are the gardener and housekeeper at the club. I love my twin sister, but I truly think she's embarrassed about my hanging out with Alicia. Alicia isn't rich and fancy like the SF2s, but I don't care. I think she's the coolest friend anyone could ever want.

"I didn't know anything about this get-together," I said to Charlie as I polished off her smoothie. "What's it for?"

"It's Saturday," Ryan chimed in. "That's party day for Charlie's friends. Oh, I forgot. So are Monday, Tuesday, Wednesday, Thursday, and Friday. Wait, I left out Sunday. That's always a good day to party."

"It's not really a party," Charlie said defensively. "It's more of a photo shoot."

"A photo shoot!" Ryan laughed. "Just because you girls stand around taking pictures of yourselves trying to look like models, does not make it a photo shoot." Then he struck a ridiculous model-like pose, sucking in his cheeks, putting his hands on his hips, and doing a stupid-looking runway walk across the deck.

I laughed, but now it was Charlie's turn not to be amused.

"For your information," she said to Ryan, "we are having an actual fashion photographer here. Lauren has arranged it all."

That shut Ryan up. Lauren Wadsworth, his sometime girlfriend, who is rich and beautiful and perfect and the most popular girl at our school, probably had her dad call up *Seventeen* magazine and send over their best fashion photographer. The Wadsworths are that kind of family—they do everything really big. Like when Lauren had her twelfth birthday party, it was at a recording studio in Hollywood and everyone got to cut a real record. The Diamond family—that's us—is much more ordinary. We don't do anything fancy. Like when Charlie and I had our twelfth birthday party, our friends made necklaces out of colored macaroni in the backyard. No kidding. Our grandma, GoGo, is a jewelry designer and she got this idea that we should all create "wearable food" when she saw an article in one of her hippie magazines about bacon bikinis.

Charlie got up from her beach lounger and gathered up her headband, sunglasses, and sunscreen from the side table.

"My friends and the photographer are going to be here in half an hour," she said to me. "So maybe you and Alicia and the new guys can hang out somewhere else."

"No problem, Charlie. I'll just say the magic words and make us all invisible."

Charlie let out a huge sigh. "I'm sorry, Sammie. I had dibs on the deck and patio. And we really don't want anyone else there. Just see if you can make that happen, all right?"

Charlie headed down the wooden path to the clubhouse and went into our bungalow, letting the screen door slam behind her. I looked over at Ryan and shook my head.

"I can't believe she still wants to be friends with those SF2 kids after the trouble they got her in," I said.

Several of the SF2s had pressured Charlie to steal a history test from the teachers' lounge to give to Lauren so she could improve her grade and get ungrounded. Charlie actually did it, and had to go on trial before the school's Honor Board. She got in really bad trouble and just got off a month's detention. If that were me, I'd never want to talk to those kids again, but Charlie claims they all said they were really sorry and swore they'd never get her in that kind of trouble again.

"Charlie wants to be accepted by them," Ryan answered. "She's not tough like you."

"What makes you think I'm tough?"

"You've got spunk, Sams. Sometimes a little too much of it, in fact. But Charlie, she's traded in her spunk to be part of the SF2s. And if you want to be one of them, you have to play by their rules. Which means no little cousins from El Salvador allowed."

"They're such snobs," I said. "I hate to think Charlie is becoming like them."

"You've got to give her credit, though, Sams. Charlie is going places in the world. She sets out to do something, and she gets it done. You and me, we're just ordinary dudes."

"I am not ordinary," I snapped, "and you're not either, Ry. You're the captain of the All-City volleyball team and I'm ... I'm ..."

"Sweaty," he said, tossing me his terry cloth wrist guard. "You might want to dab your upper lip." He tapped me under the chin and headed back out to the beach, tossing the volleyball in the air and setting it with his fingertips as he went.

When I went into the house and checked myself in the bathroom mirror, I discovered Ryan was right. I was a red-hot sweaty mess. My dark blond hair had turned that special shade of baby-poop brown it gets when it's damp, and my upper lip was doing its own impression of Niagara Falls. I took a fast shower, threw on a pair of cutoff sweats and a baggy old yellow

T-shirt, and pulled my hair into a ponytail. When I came out of the bathroom, Charlie was in our room trying on outfits, deep in concentration about what to wear to the photo shoot.

"Don't wear white," I said. "Makes everyone look ten pounds heavier."

"Then I'd look just like you," she answered, and no sooner were the words out of her mouth than she let out a little gasp. "Oh, I didn't mean it to come out that way, Sammie."

"That's okay," I said, even though it actually wasn't. "A fact is a fact. I weigh ten pounds more than you."

Actually, that fact wasn't a fact either, because I weigh almost twenty pounds more than Charlie. We're identical twins in every way except for that—if you don't count the tiny red ladybug birthmark on my upper arm or the fact that I have a freckle over my right eye and she has one over her left. But over the last couple of years, I've kind of zoomed up on the old scale while Charlie has stayed the same. It might have something to do with french fries.

I said might *because I choose to believe that french fries are not fattening if you eat them standing up.*

"Doodle," I heard GoGo call from the kitchen, "Alicia's here."

Doodle is me, at least it is in GoGo-speak. She calls Charlie Noodle, not because she's limp and slimy like a wet noodle but because she's long and willowy. Since *long* and *willowy* are not words that anyone with two eyes would use to describe me, I became Doodle. Round and roly.

Enough said.

I ran out of our tiny bedroom, across the tiny living room, and into the tiny kitchen, all in about ten steps. Our bungalow is so small that Ryan has to sleep on the foldout couch in the living room and our dad sleeps in what was once a locker room. Alicia was waiting for me at the kitchen counter, munching some taco chips that GoGo was pouring into a wicker basket.

"I thought some of my homemade chips and salsa might make our visitors from El Salvador feel welcome," GoGo said when she saw me come sprinting in. GoGo loves to make visitors from other countries feel welcome. Once, my dad had a friend visiting from France, and GoGo said *merci beaucoup* about ten thousand times even though the guy was born in Brooklyn and spoke perfect English.

"Hi," I said, giving Alicia a hug. Usually she wears her shiny black hair pulled back in a clip, but today she was wearing it down and it looked really pretty and bouncy. "So where are these new boys everyone's talking about?"

"They're on their way in," she answered. "Oscar's kind of a slowpoke. Wait until you meet them, Sammie.

They're so cute. And their faces are totally identical, just like you and Charlie."

"Wait . . . you mean I won't be able to tell them apart?"

"Oh no," Alicia said with a giggle. "You'll be able to tell them apart, no problem. Trust me on that."

That was a strange thing for Alicia to say, but before I could ask what she meant, I saw her dad, Candido, coming in from the parking lot, followed by a boy who looked to be around my age. He had golden-brown skin, long jet-black hair that flopped casually over one eye, and the whitest teeth I had ever seen. Alicia had lied—he wasn't cute, he was awesome.

"Sammie, this is my nephew Eddie," Candido said. Eddie walked right up to me, with an easy, athletic bounce in his step, and stuck out his hand. He didn't seem shy in the least.

"*Hola*," he said.

He smiled at me with those gorgeous, glistening teeth and I suddenly wished I had put on a better T-shirt. I'm not even going to go into how I felt about my cutoff sweats.

If Eddie is this handsome, I can't wait to meet his brother. After all, doesn't two of a good thing make it doubly good?

I didn't have long to wait. Oscar soon appeared, his gorgeous black hair blowing in the ocean breeze. He was wearing a supersize black T-shirt with a yellow Batman logo on the front. He had the same sparkling teeth as his brother, the same adorable smile, but there was one major difference. Something was wrong with his leg. And I don't mean a *little* something, but a *big* something.

He was limping badly as he walked over to us, so badly that it looked like he might lose his balance and fall down with every step. The foot on his left leg was all twisted around, almost facing backward, and he seemed to be walking on his ankle rather than on the bottom of his foot. I had never seen anything like that.

Okay, Sammie, do not stare at his leg. Look into his eyes.

"This is my other nephew, Oscar," Candido said proudly as Oscar stopped to catch his breath.

"Does he speak English?" I whispered to Alicia.

"*Sí*, I do," Oscar answered.

"Our uncle and cousin teach us every summer when they come to visit our country," Eddie explained. "Oscar, he is smart and learns very well."

"My leg is not so good." Oscar chuckled. "But my brain is fast like a bolt of lightning."

All of a sudden, he puffed up his chest and, raising his arms above his head, pretended like he was hurling something into the air and across the sky.

"Um . . . let me guess," I said. "You're throwing a javelin?"

"No, I am hurling a bolt of lightning," he said. "Like superheroes do in the movies."

"Oscar is a major movie fan," Alicia explained.

"If it's on a screen and flies or wears a cape, count him in."

Oscar held his hands out in front of him and flexed his muscles like the Incredible Hulk, but with no shirt-ripping involved. It was really cute, even though it was not at all what I was expecting. I don't want to sound mean here, but the guy could barely stand up, and there he was, pretending to be the Hulk or another one of the Avengers or someone.

"That's quite a move you have there," I said.

"Yeah," he said, doing it again.

Alicia and Eddie laughed, but I wasn't sure what to do. If Oscar had been regular, without that messed-up leg, I would have joined in and laughed, too. I mean, he was funny. But I didn't feel right laughing at him. What if he thought I was laughing because he was disabled? So I just kind of stood there awkwardly, not knowing what to do.

Luckily, GoGo knew exactly what to do. She picked up the tray of salsa and chips and carried it to the kitchen breakfast nook where we eat most of our meals. She placed the tray on the table and gestured to Oscar and Eddie.

"Why don't you boys have a seat and help yourselves to some chips and dip," she said. "It's our way of saying *bienvenidos*."

That's GoGo for you. Why say welcome in English if you can say it in Spanish?

Eddie slid into the booth and dug right in. It took

a little longer for Oscar to get there. As he limped the few feet across the room, I just stood there, trying not to stare at his leg. I was trying so hard to make him feel normal that I made myself feel completely uncomfortable.

"How long are you boys going to be visiting here?" GoGo asked.

"About three weeks," Eddie said.

"Oh, that's a nice long vacation."

"It's not exactly a vacation," Alicia said. "Oscar is going to have an operation on his foot. There is a doctor at Children's Hospital who specializes in fixing what he has. It's called a clubfoot."

Charlie came bouncing into the kitchen just as Alicia was finishing her sentence. She was all put-together in white jeans and a black-and-white tank top that I recognized as Lauren's.

That's right; Charlie and Lauren wear the same size. And that's right; I don't.

"Somebody say something about a club?" Charlie asked Alicia with a big smile. "Whatever it is, I want to join. I love clubs."

Ouch.

"Alicia was just explaining that her cousin Oscar has come to America to have his clubfoot corrected," GoGo said, in a voice that was unusually stern for her.

Charlie turned around and looked at the two guys sitting in our kitchen booth. Immediately, her eyes fell on Oscar's foot.

"Oh," she said. "Sorry." She shrugged and quickly looked away.

"When you boys are finished eating, maybe Charlie and Sammie can walk you out to the beach and show you around the Sporty Forty," GoGo said. "Do you like the ocean?"

"They're both good swimmers," Candido said.

"Especially Oscar," Eddie added. "He swims like a fish."

"No, I swim like Aquaman," Oscar said, making a funny fish face like he was blowing bubbles. Everyone laughed but Charlie.

"Come on, guys," I said. "Follow me. I'll introduce you to my favorite ocean."

I headed outside, with Alicia and Eddie right behind me, and Oscar trailing behind. I walked out onto the beach and waited for them to join me. It made me happy to see the expressions on their faces when they looked out at the sand and the sparkling water beyond. It really is beautiful where I live.

Charlie stood on the deck, calling my name. But just as I ran back to see what she had to say, she was interrupted by another voice. It was Lauren Wadsworth, bursting in from the parking lot in her adorable flowered turquoise sundress, her arms filled with clothes still on hangers.

"Charlie! We're here!" she called. "And wait until you see all the different outfits we brought."

Lauren was followed by three more of the Sporty

Forty girls—Brooke Addison, the gorgeous one, Jillian Kendall, the other gorgeous one, and Lily March, the other gorgeous one.

Oh, did I mention that all the SF2 girls are gorgeous?

"I just got a text from the photographer," Lauren chattered on, unaware—or not caring—that there were other people there besides herself and her friends. "He's coming in from Malibu and he'll be here in ten minutes, but he said for us to get ready. He wants to be shooting by four o'clock, which he calls the golden hour. That's when the light is best."

"And we'll all look like we have golden hair and tans," Brooke added. Apparently, she hadn't gotten the news that she already had golden hair and the world's most perfect golden tan.

"Hi, everyone," Alicia spoke up. I noticed that her tone of voice was kind of aggressive, as if to say, *I'm here, too, and the least you could do is say hello.*

"Oh, nice to see you, Alicia," Lauren said unconvincingly. "By the way, how long are you going to be here?"

"Not long," Charlie said quickly. "They just stopped by for a minute."

"Who's 'they'?" Jillian asked, flopping her armload of clothes down on one of the deck chairs.

"Us," came the answer. Eddie walked over from the sand and waved at the girls. "I'm Eddie Bermudez, Alicia's cousin."

Brooke and Lily each gave Eddie a pretty deluxe smile.

"And this is my brother, Oscar," Eddie said as Oscar hobbled across the deck and joined him.

All three girls tried not to stare at his foot, but not Lauren. Her big blue eyes traveled down his body, taking in every detail, including the bootlike shoe he wore on his left foot which was completely worn down on the outside from walking on his ankle. She didn't say a word. She didn't have to.

"We're having a photo shoot here," she whispered to Charlie. "A *glamorous* photo shoot."

"Don't worry. I'll handle this," Charlie whispered back.

Without another word, Charlie grabbed me by the arm and yanked me into the house. I didn't know exactly what she was going to say, but I knew one thing: I wasn't going to like it.

Cool Oscar

....

Chapter 2

"This is all your fault," Charlie said, slamming the door behind us so no one outside could hear.

"First of all," I shot back, "I don't even know what 'this' is. And second of all, how come everything is always *all* my fault? And third of all, your eye is doing that twitchy thing it does, which makes it very hard to concentrate on anything you're saying."

"My eye twitches when I'm mad, Sammie, you know that. And I'm really mad, so expect to see a whole lot more twitching where this is coming from."

"Here's a radical idea," I said. "Maybe you could try to make a little sense. Just a suggestion, of course."

Charlie took a deep breath. When she finally spoke, it was with a combination of annoyance and authority.

"I told you, Sammie. My friends and I are using the deck and the beach. We don't want anyone else there. I'm really upset that these new guys are interfering with our plans, and I think I have a right to be."

"You don't own the beach," I said to her. "Besides, those guys seem very nice and they're just hanging out and eating some chips. I don't get how that disrupts your glamorous photo shoot."

"We're not doing a chips commercial, Sammie. We all want to be models, and being a model has nothing to do with taco chips, or salsa, or boys with weird feet."

Charlie kind of winced when she said that. I waited for her to take it back, but she didn't.

"That's harsh, Charlie," I said at last. "And by the way, in case you didn't notice, only one of them has a weird foot."

"Whatever." Charlie sighed. "You know what I mean."

Actually, I did know what she meant, and I didn't like it one bit. I knew she didn't want Oscar there because she felt it didn't look good to her new friends. Charlie wasn't totally accepted into the SF2s yet; she was still in the auditioning phase. And hanging out with a poor kid from El Salvador with a backward foot probably wasn't the cool image she was hoping to impress her friends with. That was the hard, cold truth. I didn't say anything to Charlie, just looked her deep in the eyes. This was not the way we had been raised and she knew it.

"I know what you're thinking, Sammie," she said. "I'm sure Oscar and Eddie are really nice guys. But you have to see it my way, too. Alicia and her cousins just don't belong here right now. Did you see Lauren? She looked so annoyed that they were here. I mean, really, Sams, we've got the photographer coming, and then afterward we're going to barbecue, and Jared is even going to make a bonfire on the beach."

"Not to be a party pooper or anything," I interrupted, "but bonfires on the beach are illegal, not to mention dangerous and stupid."

"Okay, okay, we won't do that. But the point is, we have this great night planned and I want everything to go right."

"Listen to me, Charlie. Did you ever think that maybe you don't have to make everything right for the SF2 kids? Maybe they should just like you the way you are, even if you can't always be perfect for them."

"I don't need a lecture now, Sams. I just need you to understand that this is important to me."

"What do you want me to do, Charlie? Kick Eddie and Oscar out?"

"When you say it that way, it makes it sound so terrible. Just take them somewhere else. Go for a ride with Candido in his truck and show them the Venice boardwalk or the skateboard park or something. They'll like that. Please."

I agreed, reluctantly. I didn't like what Charlie was doing, and to be honest I didn't like the SF2s much either, especially after they made her cheat and steal to protect Lauren. That's not what real friends do. But she was my sister and had helped me out of a lot of jams. This was the same sister who had pretended to be me during the chicken dance contest in the first-grade talent show when I got stage fright and peed in my pants. Not to mention the time last year when she pretended to be me, called that eighth-grade creep Ronald Gruntin, and told him if he didn't stop bullying me she would report him to the principal. He backed off immediately. If she could save my butt, I guess I could save hers. Besides, I realized that if Eddie and Oscar stayed at the beach, the girls would just ignore them and make them feel bad, so what was the point of insisting that they stay?

And have I mentioned that there's this sausage stand on the Venice boardwalk that has the best homemade french fries ever? A predinner snack didn't sound half bad to me.

Charlie and I went back outside. She was all smiles as she raced over to Lauren and started browsing through the clothes she'd brought. Brooke and Jillian were busy picking out what they were going to wear, but Lily was perched on the redwood picnic table, with her feet on the bench, talking to Eddie and Oscar. Well, mostly she was talking to Eddie, but Oscar was listening and nodding.

"So where are you guys from?" she asked Eddie, twirling a strand of her curly hair around her finger to make a dreadlock that flopped down onto her forehead. On anyone else, that might have looked silly, but on Lily it looked unique and fashionable, just like everything else she wore.

"San Francisco," Eddie answered, flashing her that irresistible smile of his. "It's not as beautiful as here, but it's my town."

"Not beautiful? Are you kidding me?" Lily answered. "San Francisco is the best. I could ride on the cable cars all day. And those fresh crab cocktails at Fisherman's Wharf are to die for."

"What is a cable car?" Eddie asked, looking confused.

Lily gave him a look like his brain had turned to mashed potatoes right in front of her.

"You're from San Francisco and you don't know what a cable car is?" she asked incredulously. "That's like being from Malibu and not knowing what a surfboard is!"

Alicia laughed out loud, and Lily looked at her with a raised eyebrow.

"I don't see what's so funny," Lily said.

"You have the wrong San Francisco," Alicia explained, still giggling. "Eddie and Oscar are from San Francisco Gotera, a town in the mountains of El Salvador. No cable cars there, that's for sure. Barely any real cars. And there aren't any fresh crab cocktails either, but my Aunt Maria owns a *pupusería*, and her *pupusas* are to die for."

"Like anyone here is supposed to know what a *pupusa* is?" Lauren called out. "Sounds like something that should be in a diaper!"

Jillian and Brooke howled with laughter, and Lauren looked really pleased with herself. Personally, I haven't made a diaper joke since I was in kindergarten, and even then it was considered immature.

"It's a handmade tortilla stuffed with cheese or beans or pork," I said, feeling my face flush with anger. "Esperanza makes them for us all the time. They're delicious, especially if—"

Charlie obviously wasn't pleased with the *pupusa* turn the conversation had taken and she cut me off before I even got to describe the yummy melted cheese center of Espie's *pupusas*.

"Sammie has to go," she said. "She's taking Oscar and Eddie on a little tour of the neighborhood."

"Be sure to go to the Santa Monica mall," Jillian said. Then turning to Eddie, she explained, "There's this store called Kicks that has the most amazing vintage-style sneakers."

"I already have a pair of sneakers," Eddie said.

Jillian glanced down at the basic white sneakers Eddie was wearing.

"Oh, those," she said, and frowned. "Trust me, you need to get a pair of retro ones. It will blow your friends away when you go to your next party—"

"I hate to break this up," Charlie interrupted, "but

you guys better get going. We have to get started here if we want to catch the golden hour."

She took me by the arm and practically shoved me in the direction of the parking lot.

"Follow me, group," I said to the boys and Alicia. "I will lead you to french fries."

Candido got the keys to his truck, and we all headed to the parking lot. Eddie and Alicia were directly behind him and bringing up the rear was Oscar, doing the best he could to keep up on his bad foot.

Just as we reached Candido's beat-up red truck, a silver convertible sports car turned in from Pacific Coast Highway and screeched to a stop next to us. It was so sleek and low to the ground that it looked more like a rocket than a car. The driver was about thirty years old, with gold-rimmed aviator sunglasses sitting on his bleached-blond hair. A scarf with black skulls all over it was knotted around his neck. It didn't take much to guess who he was.

"You're the photographer, right?" I said.

"Tyler Frank," he answered, getting out of the front seat and showing off his big-time designer jeans and tattooed arms. "Are you Chip Wadsworth's daughter?"

Maybe this guy should get a prescription for those aviator glasses, because if there's one thing I don't look like, it's Chip Wadsworth's daughter. Lauren Wadsworth wouldn't be caught dead in cutoff sweats and a baggy T-shirt.

"Nope. She's inside with the other glamour girls," I said. "We're the nonglam group."

"I wouldn't be so hard on yourself," Tyler said, popping open the trunk and pulling out his camera bag. "True glamour comes in all shapes and styles."

Oscar and Eddie were gaping at Tyler's car. You don't see a car like that even in Malibu much, but for two kids from San Francisco Gotera, his Ferrari must have seemed like it was from the future.

"Is this Batman's car?" Oscar asked him.

Tyler laughed in a real friendly way.

"Nah, his is black and flies," he said. "This baby stays firmly on the ground."

"Can I look under the baby's hood?" Oscar asked.

"That's not the first question most people ask." Tyler smiled. "But hey, why not?" He popped open the hood to reveal the shiny, powerful engine inside.

"My brother, he loves cars," Eddie explained. "Our father owns a garage in El Salvador and Oscar helps him a lot."

"El Salvador, huh?" Tyler said. "I was there once. *Sports Illustrated* sent me to shoot a soccer match."

"I play soccer," Eddie said proudly.

"In our town, he is a star," Oscar added just before he dove headlong under the hood of the car.

"It's a beautiful country . . . nice people," Tyler said.

As he went on to describe how he hiked to the top of the Santa Ana Volcano, Oscar poked around in the engine. I think the kid would have camped out for a week under the hood if he could have. He got his face right down in there and looked at every hose and spark plug. (Okay, I have no idea what a spark plug is, but I'm just going to assume there were a couple somewhere in there.) Tyler watched him with curiosity, taking in everything about Oscar with a photographer's eye—his good looks, his intelligent dark eyes, and of course, his badly deformed leg. When Oscar looked up, Tyler just nodded and said, "You're a brave little dude."

"I am not a little dude," Oscar answered, pulling himself up to his full height. "But I am brave, just like the Avengers."

"The Avengers, huh?" Tyler said with a laugh. "I'm a fan, too. But listen, bro, I'm going to have to cut this conversation short. I've got to make Chip Wadsworth's little girl look good if I want to get paid for this gig."

"That won't be hard," I said. "Lauren Wadsworth always looks good. Even when she looks bad she looks good."

"Yes, *very* good," Eddie said. "Those girls at the club are so beautiful."

"Well, thanks a whole lot," Alicia said, giving him a punch in the arm. "And what are we? Chopped olives?"

"I think you mean chopped liver!" Tyler hooted. "And no, you're not! All you kids are great looking. It's just that Chip's not paying me to shoot you, so I've got to go. *Adios, muchachos.*"

He slammed down the hood of his car, slung his camera bag over his shoulder, and headed off to golden hour at the beach. As for us, we climbed into Candido's beat-up red truck and headed a couple miles down the coast to the Venice boardwalk.

The boardwalk is a totally awesome place. All kinds of people hang out there on the weekends—Rollerbladers, muscle beach bums, tourists, magicians, earring sellers. There's even a guy who juggles chain saws. No kidding. People walk along and check out the scene, eat french fries and drink smoothies, and soak up the ocean air.

We joined the throngs of people on the boardwalk. Oscar and Eddie couldn't believe the amazing sight. They took in everything, barely blinking. I knew the feeling—it was the way I felt the first time I went to Disneyland and saw a life-size Minnie Mouse walking around. I was so blown away that I actually fainted, and Minnie Mouse had to revive me. Lucky for me, she's not just another mouse who looks good in a red polka-dot dress.

The best part of our stroll was when we stopped to watch a street magician who called himself Marco the Magnificent. After doing a trick where he cut a rope in two and then put it back together, Marco called on Oscar to come up and assist him with his next trick. As Oscar limped up to the front of the crowd, he tugged at his oversize T-shirt, trying to pull it down low so you couldn't see much of his leg. A clubfoot isn't something you can cover up, though, and a couple of superbuff teenagers who had come to the beach to play basketball snickered when he passed by. He didn't even glance at them, just kept walking. If it were me, and I thought everyone was looking at my twisted leg and secretly wondering what was wrong with it, I would never leave my room.

Not Oscar. Marco asked him where he was from, and when he answered El Salvador, a bunch of people in the crowd applauded. Oscar shot them a big grin and said something in Spanish. One of the men hollered, "*Viva* El Salvador," after which Oscar did his lightning bolt thing and shouted, "*Viva* America!" The whole crowd cheered and Oscar flexed his muscles like the Hulk and took a bow.

"That boy is such a ham," Alicia said, and although she said it as a criticism, I could tell she loved him like crazy.

"No, Alicia, Oscar is not a ham," Eddie said. "He is a human."

There wasn't time to explain to him that Oscar hamming it up with Marco was not the same as the sliced stuff you eat with Swiss cheese on a sandwich. The magic trick was already underway, and Marco was attempting to pull two quarters out of Oscar's ear and one out of his nose. Oscar played along with it, squinching up his cheeks and grunting as if Marco were really making the quarters come out of his face instead of out of his sleeve. When the trick was over, Oscar was feeling so buzzed that he grabbed the microphone and let loose with a couple of superhero voices. At least, I assumed that's what they were. I mean, who else says things like "Avengers, assemble!" and "powers, activate"?

He got a big round of applause, and a lot of people slapped him on the back as he wove his way through the crowd back to us.

"How was I?" he asked Eddie.

"Alicia said you were bacon," Eddie whispered back to him.

"I Iam," she corrected. Oscar looked confused.

"You did just fine, *mijo*," Candido said to him. "I think you deserve something to eat."

We walked to the sausage stand and bought a bag of french fries to split. As we sat on one of the wooden benches, happily munching fries, our legs stretched out in front of us, a little boy carrying a helium balloon that said I'M THE MAN came up to us. He wasn't more than two years old.

"Look, Mommy," he said, pointing to Oscar's foot. "That boy has an ouchie."

The mom looked very embarrassed and picked him up quickly. As she carried him away, I heard her saying, "That's not nice, Hudson."

I glanced over at Oscar to see if he felt bad, but he didn't seem to. I tried to imagine how I'd feel if people stared at me all the time. I feel self-conscious when I get a zit. Having a clubfoot was like having a five-pound zit with blinking red lights on it. I looked at Oscar smiling and laughing with Alicia and considered how much inner strength it took for him to have such a great outlook on life.

Alicia was talking nonstop to both boys, blabbering on in Spanish, waving her hands around in the air. Every once in a while, she'd turn to me and give me a quick translation. She was trying to explain why a person would juggle chain saws, which is no easy thing to explain in any language, when you think about it. When she stopped for a breath, I took the opportunity to interrupt.

"So what do you think of Venice?" I asked Oscar and Eddie.

"It's like the outdoor market at home," Oscar said. "Only no mangoes."

"And with lots more girls in bikinis," Eddie observed.

"My brother, all he thinks about is girls," Oscar said to me.

"No, Oscar. I think about soccer, too," he said, patting his blue-and-white soccer jersey. "Girls first, soccer second, food third, sleep fourth."

"School last," Oscar added.

"I'm not smart like you," Eddie snapped.

"I'm not fast like you," Oscar snapped back.

Then they said a few words to each other in Spanish. I couldn't understand what they were saying, but I knew exactly what was going on with them. It's hard when you're twins. You try not to be competitive, but everyone is always comparing you to each other, so it's really hard not to be. Like with Charlie and me. She's thin, I'm not. I'm funny, she's not. She's quick, I'm strong. She's fashionable, I'm sloppy. She's cool, I'm sort of a dork. No matter how hard we try, we are always measuring ourselves against each other. And here were Oscar and Eddie doing the same thing, which wasn't really fair because Oscar was born with a major disadvantage. At least that's how I saw it.

We stayed on the boardwalk for another half hour, just hanging out and talking. Oscar described their house in San Francisco Gotera—two white plaster rooms in the back of a little restaurant their mom ran. At night, Oscar would do his homework in the restaurant while his mom cooked for the customers and his dad took Eddie to play at the soccer field. Then Oscar would take out his colored pencils and spend the rest of the night drawing superheroes. He must have been a very good artist, because he told me he even painted a mural of the Avengers on the wall of the restaurant. When I asked what his town was like, he told me about the big adobe church in the square that was cool in summer and smelled like incense and candle wax. It was where he and Eddie had been baptized, and where his mom went to pray for his leg to heal. He described fun Sunday rides on his dad's motor scooter over the dusty roads to the river, where they'd swim and catch tadpoles. Eddie didn't talk much, but then, it's hard to talk when your tongue is hanging out over every pretty girl who walks by.

We talked until the sky was beginning to fade into the hazy lavender of dusk. I felt like I had known Oscar for much longer than just a couple of hours.

"We should get back to the club now," Candido said. "It will be dark soon."

Oscar didn't want to leave, but Eddie was all for it.

"Let's go visit the girls," he said. "I think Lily, she likes me."

"You think every girl likes you," Oscar said.

"That's because it's true."

Alicia and I exchanged a worried look.

"I'm going to explain how it works here," she whispered to me, then took Eddie by the arm and walked ahead of us as we headed for the truck. I saw that she was talking to him in a very serious tone. He listened to her, then just laughed and walked on ahead.

"What did you say to him?" I asked as she rejoined Oscar and me.

"I told him that those girls at the beach club are very rich," she explained. "And that the boys they like come from rich families with fancy cars and big houses."

"And what did he say?"

"He laughed and said that they hadn't met Eddie Bermudez yet."

That was a worrisome thought. Eddie didn't know those SF2 kids. They came from an entirely different world, and they didn't exactly welcome outsiders. I could vouch for that from personal experience. They kind of accepted Charlie because she worked so hard at being liked. But the minute I became friends with Alicia, they wrote me off as worthless.

As we headed back to Candido's truck, I watched Oscar and Eddie stop to look at the last of the surfers riding the waves in.

"Is Oscar always so sweet and friendly?" I asked Alicia.

She shook her head. "I've never seen him like this before. He's always funny, but he usually doesn't talk this much. He spends most of his time drawing because he wants to be a comic book artist someday. As you can see, he loves all that stuff."

"What a cool thing to want to be," I said.

Alicia was quiet for a minute. When she spoke, she seemed to be carefully selecting her words.

"I think he likes you, Sammie," she said in a serious tone.

"I like him, too," I answered. "He's hilarious ... and obviously really talented."

She turned to me and took my hand, a worried look on her face. "Oscar has been through a lot. He has a very tender heart."

"What are you saying, Alicia?"

"I'm just saying be careful," she said. "He means a lot to me."

I wasn't sure what she meant by that, but before I could ask she had run off to watch the sunset with her cousins.

Two Parties

....

Chapter 3

"Hey, look who finally decided to show up," Ryan said as we walked in from the parking lot and pushed open the gate to the beach club. "What took you so long?"

"We got some fries at Jody's Sausage Stand," I said.

"What? And you didn't bring any back for your favorite brother?"

"Ryan, you're my *only* brother."

"Which makes me automatically your favorite. Isn't that right, guys?" he said, giving Oscar and Eddie a punch in the arm.

Even though they had never met before, Eddie and Oscar immediately punched Ryan right back, and the three of them cracked up. I don't know what it is with boys, what makes them think a slug in the arm is an invitation to be best friends. I mean, if someone punches me, I want to punch them back twice as hard.

Ryan threw his arm around Eddie's shoulder.

"Hey, I'm Ryan. And I have to tell you that if I hear one more, 'That looks adorable on you,' my head just might explode off my neck."

Oscar looked very concerned.

"What is the problem with his head?" he leaned over and whispered.

"Nothing," I answered. "Unless you consider missing a brain a problem."

"Oh, that sounds very serious," Oscar said, looking suddenly sad. "Your poor brother."

He clutched his heart. I felt terrible. Obviously, he hadn't gotten my sarcasm.

"Oh no, Oscar," I hurried to add, remembering Alicia's warning about his tender heart. "He really does have a brain. I was just kidding."

I looked at Oscar and saw that he was laughing hysterically. He was the one who had played a joke on me!

"Very funny!" I said, and pushed him playfully. (That was a push, not a punch.) I thought he was going to push me back, but he didn't. He put his arm around me instead. That was a total surprise. My dad puts his arm around me when we walk along the boardwalk to get ice cream cones. And Ryan puts his arm around me when he's trying to get me to clear the table on his night. But Oscar was the first boy my age to ever put his arm around me in a serious kind of way. I didn't know if he was trying to be romantic, or if that's just the kind of thing people do in El Salvador when they're being friendly. It made me feel weird and uncomfortable. I could feel myself get all tense around the shoulder area. He must have felt it, too, because he took his arm down right away.

Ryan, who makes friends as easily as fish swim in water, had already buddied up with Eddie.

"We could use some guy energy here," he was saying to him as we made our way onto the deck. "This is what I've had to listen to for the last two hours."

Raising his voice about two octaves, he started doing a series of impressions that actually sounded a lot like Lauren, Jillian, Brooke, and Lily.

"How cute is this top!" he squealed.

"OMG, you look totally awesome in that."

"Is there lip gloss on my teeth?"

"Does this make me look too fat?"

"Does this make me look too skinny?"

Then he dropped the squeaky voices and pretended to be barfing, collapsing in a heap on the wooden deck in front of us. Eddie looked a little startled, but Oscar had already caught on to Ryan's twisted sense of humor.

"You are very funny," he said. "I hate to leave, but now I am going to take a ride in Tyler's Batman car."

"You're out of luck, dude," Ryan said. "He

vamoosed. The poor guy went running out of here as soon as he finished taking their pictures. I think if he heard one more "OMG," his ears would have shriveled up and dropped right off."

"Where did the girls go?" Eddie asked, looking out onto the beach but seeing only the shadowy outline of my dad on the sand next to the volleyball court, lighting the barbecue.

"They're inside, changing back into their regular clothes."

"We were, but we decided not to," Lauren called, strutting out onto the deck from inside the kitchen. "We wanted to wait and show Sammie and Alicia and Eddie our top-model look."

Boy, that made me mad.

"Excuse me, Lauren," I blurted out, "but there's another person here, and his name is Oscar."

"You don't have to get all huffy, Sammie. I see him. I'm not blind." Then she looked a little startled and glanced at Oscar. "No offense to disabled people."

Really? Did she just say that? Yes, she actually did.

Lauren was wearing jeans so tight they looked like they were sprayed on and a gold shimmery top the exact color of her gold sandals and huge gold hoop earrings. Even I, who am not a Lauren Wadsworth fan, had to admit she looked unbelievably great. She seemed so glamorous that I was really surprised when she stuck two fingers into her mouth and let out a loud guy-size whistle. Where did *that* come from?

"Top models," she called. "Report to the runway."

One by one, the girls came out doing their runway walks. Jillian had on so much eye makeup I was surprised she could even hold her eyelids up. Brooke had gone for the military look in honor of her boyfriend, the General (who, by the way, isn't one, but they call him that anyway because he always wears camouflage pants). She was in cutoff camouflage shorts with high-heeled pumps, which I'm pretty sure are not the best shoe choice if you're in actual battle. As always, Lily looked the most original. She wore a slouchy knit beanie that went halfway down her back and breezy, beachy, striped pants rolled up to the knee.

"You look *muy bonita*," Eddie said to her. "Which in my language means—"

"I know what it means." Lily smiled at him. "I've been taking Spanish since sixth grade. I can even sing a song in Spanish."

She burst into a little chorus of "La Bamba," and Eddie joined in. If you ask me, this was turning into a major flirt fest.

The last one out was my sister, Charlie, whose smile was so big I thought her face was going to crack. She was wearing a totally glammed-up version of a tennis outfit with platform tennis shoes, white shorts, and a white tube top. She carried her racket in one hand and a wide-brimmed straw hat in the other. It was clear that whoever put that outfit together had never touched a tennis racket in her life. I could tell Lauren had picked out those clothes. After a couple of serves, a tube top like that would be around your ankles, particularly if you were small on the boob front, like Charlie.

Okay, I admit it. Mine are a little bigger. I'm not bragging, just saying that things like that are bound to happen when you weigh twenty pounds more than your twin.

"You guys all look great," Alicia, who is the sweetest person in the world, said when they were all lined up in front of us. "Can we see the pictures?"

"We won't have them until tomorrow." Jillian could barely get the words out because she was so occupied trying to adjust one of her false eyelashes that seemed to be crawling like a caterpillar down the side of her face.

"Tyler is photoshopping them," Brooke went on. "Just to clean up any little imperfections. That's what they do with all cover girls, you know."

"They don't always do that," Lily commented, and she should know because she's actually been a model for the Gap catalog.

"You are so wrong, Lily," Jillian responded in a huffy voice. "I read that in *Popstar Daily* so I know it's true."

Jillian is obsessed with reality television stars. When the rest of us are doing algebra problems, she's poring over celebrity gossip magazines. Just the other day, I heard her telling Charlie that gossip magazines are a lot more relevant to her life than knowing the value of *x*—which is a stupid letter, anyway.

"Girls, focus," Lauren said. "The important thing is that Tyler said he thinks some of us have real model potential." I noticed that she directed her remark to Ryan. "Just think, Ry. This could be the start of my career."

"I'm more interested in the start of dinner," my always-starving brother answered. "Hey, Dad," he bellowed, "how long before we eat?"

"The fire's not hot enough yet," he called back. "Why don't you kids play some volleyball until the burgers are ready?"

"Oh, I just love beach volleyball," Lauren said.

Okay, I happen to know that she not only doesn't *love* beach volleyball, she doesn't even *like* it. She never ever plays when Ryan's not there—she just lies there in the sun, rotating herself like a chicken on a spit. But everyone knows that the fastest way to my brother's heart is either through food or sports . . . and since my dad was in charge of the burgers, Lauren picked sports.

"I have an idea," Lily said. "What if Eddie stays for dinner and volleyball? It could be all of us versus Ryan and Eddie. Girls against guys. That'd be fun."

I couldn't believe what I was hearing. She was inviting Eddie right in front of Oscar, without even thinking about how that would make Oscar feel. I knew how he must have felt—left out. The SF2s are experts at making you feel that way. I have the personal experience to prove it.

I glanced at Oscar to see if his face showed anything. He was looking down at the deck as though he'd suddenly developed a major interest in wooden planks.

"What about Oscar?" Eddie said. "He can't play but he can keep score . . . and eat."

"Yeah, bro. You're welcome to stay," Ryan said.

I wanted to reach out and hug both of them for doing just what brothers are supposed to do, but their kindness and attention seemed to embarrass Oscar even more.

"That's okay," he said. "I'm not that hungry."

"Good, then it's settled," Lauren said, quickly seizing the opportunity to exclude him. I could hear the relief in her voice. "Eddie, get your game face on. We'll go inside and change and meet you guys on the beach in five minutes."

The girls ran inside, and Ryan and Eddie went out onto the beach to warm up. I could see right away that Eddie was going to be a great player. He could jump really high, his hands were quick, and he had the graceful moves of a natural athlete. My heart ached for Oscar. I wondered how many moments like this he had suffered, watching his star brother do everything he wanted to do but couldn't. Alicia reached out and took his hand.

"Soon you'll have the surgery," she said. "And then you'll be able to run and play like everyone else."

Oscar nodded and forced a smile.

"I have a thought," I said when I couldn't stand the silence any longer. "Let's hang out together and do something else. Something really fun."

"Great idea, Sammie," Alicia said. "I know that Sara invited a couple of the Truth Tellers over for a pizza and movie night. I'll call her. I'm sure it's fine if we come."

"What's a Truth Teller?" Oscar asked.

"It's a club at school that Sammie and I and Sara Berlin and a bunch of other kids belong to," Alicia explained. "We all get together to tell the truth about how we feel."

Oscar looked perplexed. "Why do you need a club to tell the truth?"

"We do performances and stuff, based on our true feelings," I tried to explain. "We even performed at a city council meeting and got a standing ovation."

Alicia said something to Oscar in Spanish. I assumed she was telling him more about the Truth Tellers, although from the look on his face, he didn't seem too clear on the concept. I could relate. My dad still doesn't get the concept of Truth Tellers, and he's forty-five and not from El Salvador.

"I'm going inside to call Sara," Alicia said. "Be back in a sec."

Oscar and I sat down on a couple of the wooden deck chairs. He looked out at the sand, watching Ryan and Eddie jump in the air and practice spiking the ball over the net.

"Eddie can jump really high, like a frog," he said.

"More like a flea," I answered. "Did you know that fleas can jump one hundred times their body size?"

"I will tell that to my dog when I get home," Oscar said, and we both burst out laughing.

That smile, it was good to see it back.

"Hey, youngsters," a booming voice called out. I turned around to see Tom Ballard pushing open the gate, followed by his son, Spencer. The Ballards are Sporty Forty members, and although Charlie doesn't talk about it much, I know she really likes Spencer, which is okay with me, because of all the SF2 guys, I think he's the nicest. And that cute dimple on his cheek doesn't hurt, either.

"Hello, Mr. Ballard," I said, getting to my feet to shake his hand. I don't always shake hands with grown-ups, but Mr. Ballard is on the Santa Monica City Council, and since he's always campaigning for re-election, he is a major handshaker. Every time I see him, he grabs my hand and pumps it so hard I feel like I should be spitting up water.

"Nice to see you, young lady," he said, grabbing my hand with his firm grip and starting to pump. "Which one of Rick's girls are you again?"

"That's Sammie, Dad," Spencer said.

"One day I'll learn to tell you two apart," Mr. Ballard said with his big, friendly laugh.

"It's not that hard, Dad."

I wondered what Spencer meant by that. Did he mean that you could tell it was me from my vibrant personality and enormous personal charm? Or did he mean that you could tell it was me because I'm fatter than Charlie?

I'm hoping for the first, guys, but I'm betting it's the second.

"Who's your good-looking pal?" Mr. Ballard asked, as Oscar rose to his feet.

"This is Oscar Bermudez," I said. "He's from El Salvador."

Mr. Ballard grabbed Oscar's hand and shook it vigorously.

"Welcome to our shores," Mr. Ballard said. "What brings you here?"

"An American doctor came to my town," Oscar said. "He says he can fix my foot, so he helped me come to Los Angeles to have an operation."

"Oh, at Children's Hospital?" Mr. Ballard asked.

Oscar nodded.

"Excellent institution," Mr. Ballard said. "It's in my district. Who's the doctor?"

"Dr. Mandel is his name, but I call him Dr. Superpower."

"Ah, yes," Mr. Ballard said with a laugh. "Very appropriate. Al Mandel is a super guy. A member of our club and a pretty good golf player, too. He's got a five handicap."

"No sir, I am the one with the handicap," Oscar said.

Mr. Ballard let out a huge laugh and slapped Oscar on the back.

"I like your sense of humor," he said. "In the meantime, Sammie, where is your grandmother? I'm having a fund-raiser here next weekend, and I want to see if she'll whip up some of those chicken skewers and cheesy thingamajigs she's so famous for."

"She's in the kitchen," I answered.

"I bet she's slicing cantaloupe," Spencer said, pretending to be looking in the kitchen but craning his neck to see if he could spot Charlie in the house. "She always does that for parties."

"Great!" Mr. Ballard said. "Sliced cantaloupe is a real vote-getter in my book."

"Sara says we're good for tonight," Alicia shouted as she came running out of the kitchen. "Oscar, you're going to meet the Truth Tellers."

"The Truth Tellers!" Mr. Ballard said, reaching out to shake Alicia's hand vigorously. "I remember that group. You kids performed at the city council open meeting. You were great. Real crowd-pleasers."

"Thank you, sir," Alicia said. I was surprised to see that she suddenly got shy, but then, Mr. Ballard is a big man with a big voice and a big personality. He can be intimidating.

"Say, what are you kids doing next Saturday?" he asked. "I'm having a fund-raiser here and I'd love to have you perform. I'm raising money for the schools' arts programs. We have to make up for those budget cuts, and you guys might help motivate people to give. What do you say?"

"Dad, do you have to put everyone to work raising money for one of your causes?" Spencer said, embarrassed by his father's larger-than-life behavior.

"As a matter of fact, I do," Mr. Ballard said, letting out a big, friendly laugh. "We all care about our schools. We all need to pitch in. So . . . what do you say, ladies?"

"We'd love to," Alicia answered. "Wouldn't we, Sammie?"

"Well, we'd have to ask Ms. Carew first. She's our teacher."

"How could she say no?" Alicia added quickly. "This is a big chance for us to be seen, and to do something important at the same time."

"It's settled then," Mr. Ballard said. "Next Saturday. Here at the club. Six thirty. I know you'll come up with something great to help out the schools. Maybe we can even contribute something to this young man's recuperation. Now, where's that grandma of yours?"

Without waiting for an answer, he hustled off toward the kitchen, passing Charlie and the girls as they streamed outside.

"Hi there, Sammie," he said, and waved to Charlie.

Spencer laughed, and I caught a short but wonderful glimpse of his dimple.

"That's my dad," he said. "He's got a way of knowing everybody and knowing nobody at the same time."

"That's an interesting observation," I began, but then noticed that Spencer had already left my side and was hurrying over to Charlie and the other girls, leaving me standing there with my interesting observation dangling in midair.

You could say I felt like a total idiot, and you'd be right.

So there we were, the three of us—Oscar, Alicia, and me—definitely feeling like outsiders in my own home. I heard a horn and turned to see Ben Feldman getting out of his dad's Mercedes, dressed in his usual plaid Bermuda shorts, leather flip-flops, and polo shirt with the collar popped up.

"Text from Jared," he said, waving his cell phone at me. "He says there's a volleyball game starting."

Without another word, he blew by us and found Spencer and the SF2 girls. Together, moving like a single unit, they all headed out to the beach volleyball court. As they passed, no one stopped to ask if we wanted to join in.

But that was okay, because we didn't.

We had our own party to go to.

One of Us

....

Chapter 4

"Oh, crud! It's only you!" Sara Berlin said, throwing open the front door to her apartment. "We thought you were the pizza!"

"Sorry to disappoint you," Alicia said as we stood there in the hallway. "If I put some pepperoni on my face, would that help?"

"One hundred percent!" Sara laughed.

"Come in, kids," Sara's mother yelled from inside. "Sara, where are your manners?"

Four members of our Truth Tellers group were gathered in the living room. Bernard of the red hair, Keisha of the black hair, Etta of the green-streaked hair, and Will Lee of the short hair. Actually, everything about Will is short, but maybe that's because he's only in the sixth grade. He's hoping for a seventh-grade growth spurt. When we do our Truth Teller monologues, he talks a lot about how annoying it is to be short, especially because he always has crushes on the tallest girls in class. Nobody laughs at him, though. We just reassure him that good things come in small packages.

Sara's mom was at the kitchen counter pouring pink lemonade into red plastic cups and handing them, one at a time, to Sara's little brother, Timmy, so he could serve the guests. I had never met him, but Sara had told us in Truth Tellers that he is autistic. As soon as we came in, Timmy walked up to me and handed me a cup. Then he saw Oscar and stared at his leg a long minute. Without a word, he took the cup away from me and handed it to him.

"*Gracias*," Oscar said, taking the lemonade.

"Drink it!" Timmy said, jumping up and down and clapping his hands. "It will make your leg all better."

Oscar took a big swig as Timmy watched him, fascinated.

"*Delicioso*," Oscar said. "Now I am stronger than Iron Man." That seemed to make Timmy happy, and he skipped back to his mom to get another cup.

"Everybody, this is my cousin Oscar from El Salvador!" Alicia said, holding out her hand to introduce Oscar like he was the star of the show. "He's here to get an operation that we hope will fix his clubfoot."

There was a chorus of hellos from everyone in the

room, except Will. He walked up to Oscar to shake his hand.

"*Buenas días*," he said. "Oh, wait, that means good morning. Sorry. Maybe I should just stick to Korean." Then he bowed to Oscar and said, "*Ahn-nyung.*"

Oscar bowed right back at him and repeated, "*Ahn-nyung*," and they high-fived. It occurred to me how different this welcome was from the way Oscar was greeted by the SF2s. In Sara's house, nobody stared at him, nobody frowned at him, nobody made snide remarks, and nobody judged him. I was so proud of my friends; I just wanted to slobber all over them.

Okay, you're right. Slobbering is for dogs. Maybe just a few hugs would do.

"Listen up. I have a major announcement to make," Alicia said. "We just got invited to perform at Councilman Ballard's fund-raiser at the Sporty Forty next Saturday night . . . to raise money for the arts programs in our schools."

"Wow," Keisha said. "How cool is that?!"

"I am definitely going to add some pink to my hair for the occasion." Etta grinned. "Show those folks what some cutting-edge hair art looks like."

"And I know exactly what I'll talk about," Bernard said. "How music changed my life—and I'll do it to a drum beat."

He pulled out his drumsticks, which he always carries in his back pocket, and started tapping out a reggae rhythm on the arm of his chair. Mrs. Berlin looked up from the lemonade and gave him a look—you know the one, that special look parents give when you're about to destroy their personal property.

"I don't want to dampen your musical enthusiasm," she said, "but that's called a chair. It's used for sitting in."

"Sorry," Bernard answered, putting his drumsticks back into his pocket. "I got carried away."

Bernard gets carried away a lot. We're all used to it, but I guess Mrs. Berlin wasn't.

We decided to call Ms. Carew, our faculty sponsor whose room we meet in every Monday after school, to ask her permission to do the fund-raiser. Most teachers won't ever give you their cell phone numbers, but Ms. Carew isn't like most teachers. "This makes me so proud and happy," she said when we got her on the phone. "I'll send out an e-mail tonight to all the Truth Tellers, asking them to prepare something very special for the evening."

She said congratulations to each of us, and when she got to me, I introduced her by phone to Oscar. Just before she hung up, she suggested we do an Acceptance Circle for Oscar. It's something we do whenever there is a new person at one of our Truth Teller meetings. So we sat down in a circle and Keisha began.

"Welcome to Truth Tellers," she said to Oscar, giving him a friendly grin. Keisha has a mouthful of braces, and in school, she tries not to smile because

Jared and Sean think it's funny to call her Metal Mouth. But at Truth Tellers, she lets it all hang out. We don't care how much metal she has in her mouth.

"I think we should go around the circle and each say a word that describes Oscar," she suggested. We call this First Impression, and it's one of our favorite exercises to make a new person feel at home.

I remembered when I went to my first Truth Teller meeting and they did First Impression with me. At the time, I thought they were totally bonkers. I had never heard of an exercise to loosen up your emotions and help you discover your true feelings. Back then, the only exercises I knew were stretches to loosen up my hamstrings. A lot had changed in just two months. Now, playing First Impression seemed totally normal, and I knew the exact word I wanted to begin with. It was just the right one for Oscar.

"Brave," I said without hesitation.

"Artistic," Alicia added.

"Handsome," Etta commented, smoothing back her green-streaked hair with a hand clustered with silver and turquoise rings.

"Overcoming," Bernard said, "which may not technically be a word to describe someone, but we all know what I mean."

"Tall," Will said. Of course, Oscar wasn't tall, but when you're as height-obsessed as Will is, you measure everyone against yourself. I could tell Oscar liked being called tall, because he reached out and gave Will a friendly punch on the arm. Poor Will, it nearly knocked him over.

"I like this game," Oscar said when everyone had finished. "Okay," he continued, getting into the spirit of things. "Here I go. Bernard, you are musical. Will, you are funny. Etta, you are colorful. Keisha, you are smiling. Sara, you are curly."

Everyone laughed. Sara has this huge head of black curly hair that poofs out around her face like a lion's mane. There is no doubt that she is curly.

Then Oscar looked at me and thought for a long minute.

"Sammie," he said softly. "You are beautiful and bright like a star."

I could feel myself blush. There was so much emotion in his voice. The room got really quiet while I searched for something to say. I wanted to let him know how much his words meant to me, but I was also embarrassed, and to be honest, a little overwhelmed. No boy had ever told me I was beautiful before except Julian LaBonge, and he only said it because we were acting out a scene from *Romeo and Juliet* and it was right there on page 16 of the play. Alicia's warning for me to be careful and to not hurt Oscar echoed in my mind. I couldn't come up with the right balance of saying something nice but not saying something too nice.

Thankfully, the front door opened and Sara's father came bursting in carrying two pizza boxes.

I was so relieved. He couldn't have arrived at a better time.

"One pepperoni and one pineapple-olive-green pepper!" he called out cheerily.

Pineapple-olive-green pepper? Seriously? We all knew right away who the culprit was. Bernard. He has never ordered a regular-sounding pizza in his life. We can always count on him to order weird things, like the shrimp-anchovy-garlic combo, or spinach, almonds, and apricots.

"Were you absent on the day they handed out taste buds?" Sara asked him.

"Don't judge it until you've tried it," Bernard snapped back.

"In general, that's a good life rule," Mr. Berlin said, putting the boxes on the dining room table. "Although, I'm not so sure it applies here. There's a mighty powerful aroma coming out of that box."

We tore open the boxes and dug in. I did take a slice of the pineapple-olive-green pepper, and I'm here to tell you it is just as bad as it sounds. Don't try it at home, kids. Oscar took one bite and looked like he wanted to spit it out.

"Is this what you eat in America?" he whispered to me.

"Only if your name is Bernard."

"Good. Then I'm glad my name is Oscar."

After the pizza, we watched a really bad, but in a good kind of way, old movie called *Zombie High*

School. Afterward, we had a Who Can Do the Weirdest Zombie Walk contest. I love it that the Truth Tellers always come up with such fun and creative things to do. When it was Oscar's turn, he put some tomato sauce from the pizza box on his face so it looked like blood, crossed his eyes, and limped around the room, walking into walls. We all laughed hysterically.

"See, my bad leg is good for something," he said.

Then he lurched around the room some more, his arms out in front of him, making zombie sounds. The more he bumped into furniture, the more he moaned and groaned, the more we howled. By the end of the night, no one even had a thought about his clubfoot or his limp. He was just Oscar, King of the Zombies.

And one of us.

Ruined Plans

....

Chapter 5

"That was the best party ever," I said to Alicia as we waited in front of Sara's apartment for my dad to come pick us up.

"I like your friends," Oscar said. "They're *loco*."

"Wait. Doesn't that mean crazy?"

"Yes," he said. "But it's fun to be crazy."

"I'm glad you like everyone," Alicia said, "because we're getting together again tomorrow."

Just before the party ended, Etta had invited us all to her family picnic the next day at Mar Vista Park. Her family is Greek, and she told us that once a year they have this blowout picnic where they barbecue a whole lamb and her uncles do crazy Greek folk dances and shout "Opa!" That sounded totally fun, and we all agreed to meet at the park at noon.

When my dad pulled up, Eddie was already in the backseat. Alicia and I climbed in next to him, and Oscar sat up front. As we drove over to Alicia's apartment to drop everyone off, Eddie talked nonstop, half in Spanish and half in English. He was in a great mood. He reported that he had the best time ever at Charlie's beach barbecue, which he didn't really need to say because his face said it all. He was glowing like one of those neon bracelets the SF2s give out at all their parties.

"Lily is a beautiful girl," he said, flashing his gorgeous grin. "She likes me, too."

"How do you know?" Oscar asked.

"A man knows these things," he answered, trying to look serious and grown-up and sexy. We all hooted with laughter at that, which made him really mad.

"You will see that I am right," he said, and then he pouted all the way home. It was okay, though, because Alicia and I went right on talking about our plans for the next day. Alicia said she would ask Candido to drive us to Mar Vista Park, and I said I'd make tuna sandwiches in case we didn't want to eat a barbecued lamb, which we both agreed sounded marginally gross.

"Hold your horses," my dad interrupted. "You're not going to any picnic tomorrow."

"Dad! Everyone is. It's going to be really fun."

"Well, you're not everyone."

Oh boy, I'm hating the sound of where this is going.

"I got a call from the Sand and Surf Club today," he

went on. "They're sponsoring a round-robin tomorrow in the Under-14 category. I said you and Charlie would play."

"But, Dad, you didn't even ask me. I have plans."

"Plans can be canceled. This is important. Anna Kozlov and Marjorie Shin are coming in from San Diego to play."

"I don't care if they're coming in from Mars."

"Watch your tone, young lady. You and Charlie are going to face them in the divisional tournament in a week, and it's an excellent opportunity for a practice match."

"I'm not interested in the divisional tournament."

"Really? When it comes time for a college scholarship, I think you'll care. I'm looking at the big picture, Sammie. Tennis is your ticket to college."

It always came down to this. My dad is obsessed with Charlie and me becoming state champions or world champions. Now that I mention it, he wouldn't mind if we became champions of the whole entire galaxy. I used to love tennis, but since I've made new friends, I want to do other things. I don't want to spend four hours every day on the court, smacking balls around. Why couldn't he realize that?

"This isn't fair, Dad."

"Who says life is fair?"

That's the line he uses whenever he wants to end a conversation. He doesn't expect an answer because there's really no comeback to that question. He just says it to be annoying, and it's his way of saying, "This discussion is over." I could feel tears welling up in my eyes.

Stupid, stupid, stupid tennis. I wish the stupid game had never been invented.

We were stopped at a red light and my dad flicked on the radio, just to emphasize that the discussion was over. He tapped his fingers on the steering wheel in time to some Bruce Springsteen song on the oldies station. Oscar looked straight ahead. I'm sure he was uncomfortable sitting up there with my dad and overhearing our argument. I always hate it when I'm at a friend's house and they get in a fight with their parents. It's so uncomfortable for everyone.

Alicia put her arm around my shoulder.

"I hate tennis," I muttered.

"No, you don't," she said. "You're really good at it."

"So what? You're really good at topic sentences, but you don't have to spend all day Sunday writing them."

"Wow, Sammie, that was one crazy thought."

"I'm just so frustrated."

"I tell you what," she said as the light changed and we turned down Venice Boulevard to her apartment. "How about if we come and watch you play tomorrow? Eddie, have you ever been to a tennis tournament?"

He shook his head.

"See? It'd be a new experience for them, and it'd be really fun."

"How can you come? You and Oscar are going to the Greek picnic."

"I want to come watch you, Sammie," Oscar said from the front seat.

"We'll bring tamales and have our own picnic right there at the club," Alicia offered.

"You mean you would skip Etta's family picnic?"

"Sure," she said. "If you can't go, we won't either."

That's what a real friend is, folks. Now you know why I just love that Alicia Bermudez.

When we pulled up in front of her apartment, she gave me a hug and said they'd have Candido drop them at the Sand and Surf Club around noon. My dad told them he'd leave passes for them at the front gate, because the Sand and Surf is a pretty fancy place and doesn't let anyone in who isn't a member.

When we got home, all the lights were out, and Ryan was sprawled out on the foldout couch in the living room, his long legs hanging off the bed like one of those test dummies you see in car-crash TV ads. I tiptoed by him, and just as I passed his head, he sprang up like a jack-in-the-box and yelled, "GOTCHA!" I nearly jumped out of my skin.

"What is wrong with you?" I screamed at him.

"Come on, Sams. You have to admit it was funny."

"Yeah, funny if you're five years old. Oh, wait. Make that four. Five-year-olds would think it was stupid."

"Charlie didn't think it was funny, either." He sighed. "You two used to be so much fun. What happened?"

"We're almost thirteen," I tried to explain to him. "We don't think it's funny when you pop out of bed and scare people. And while we're on the subject, it wasn't funny at lunch the other day when you stuck a pencil up your nose and pretended to sneeze it out."

"Lauren laughed. She thought it was hilarious."

"I rest my case," I snorted and walked into my bedroom, leaving him to ponder that remark.

Charlie was in bed when I came in.

"What was all that about?" she asked, turning on the light next to our beds. Since our room is so small, our beds are really close to each other. The only thing between them is a tiny white wicker table with a night-light shaped like a tennis racket. I'll bet you'll never guess who gave that to us.

Yup, that would be our tennis-fanatic dad. It goes with the tennis ball erasers he's been getting us for our pencils since we were, like, three.

"It was just Ryan being an idiot," I said. "What else is new?"

"Yeah, he tried the jack-in-the-box thing on me, too. I told him that would have been funny if I was five."

"I said the same thing!"

It was common for Charlie and me to say the same thing at the same time. They say that identical twins have a special mind connection, and I think that may be true. When we were little, we were in a twin study that the University of California sponsored to see if we had a special language that only the two of us could understand. I don't think they proved that we did, but we liked going because they always gave us Tootsie Pops and fruit punch. In matters of refreshments, Charlie and I always thought alike.

"How was your night?" I asked her.

"Fantastic. Our team didn't win because Ben Feldman was on fire. You know Ryan, he hates losing so he got a little temperamental, which bummed Lauren out. But then at the barbecue, he ate massive quantities of food and that cheered him up. And guess what, Sams? Spencer sat next to me and told me I smelled better than his hickory burger."

I sat down on the bed next to her.

"That's pretty romantic," I said. "You really like him, huh?"

She nodded.

"I just feel so comfortable around him," she said. "He really listens when I talk. Ben's pretty cool, too. Maybe he'd like you, if you gave him a chance."

I thought of how Ben had waved his cell phone at me on the way in to the club. I don't think he even glanced at me for a nanosecond. I'm no expert on body language or anything, but that sure didn't look like *like* to me.

"I'm pretty sure he's not interested," I said. "But it's great that you and Spencer are having a good time."

I meant that. At least Charlie had picked the

nicest one of the SF2 boys. Spencer seemed almost regular, not like those superjocks Sean "I'm Cool" Patterson or Jared "I Wear My Basketball Shorts Two Sizes Too Big" McCain who only care about looking cool and making snide comments to kids they think won't stand up to them.

"Lauren says she thinks Spencer might ask me to the football game at Santa Monica High. His brother is the quarterback."

"You and Lauren getting along?" I asked. I was kind of hoping she would say no.

"Perfectly. She said she thinks I'd make a really good model."

"I didn't know you wanted to be a model. I thought you wanted to be a pediatrician."

"I used to, but being a model sounds so much more glamorous. The photographer said he thinks I have promise, and he's going to take some more shots next time he sees me."

"You mean Tyler? He's coming back?"

"Yup. Spencer's dad hired him to take pictures Saturday at the fund-raiser. Lauren thinks we could maybe get our pictures in *Los Angeles* magazine. She's going to buy a copy tomorrow, and we're all going to check out the party pages."

"Speaking of tomorrow, did Dad tell you he signed us up to play a round-robin at the Sand and Surf Club?"

"Yes. It won't be so bad, though, because Lauren

is going to come with a bunch of the girls. Brooke and Jillian, probably. And Jared said he's going to be there, too."

"Yeah, about that. Some of my friends are coming, too."

Charlie sat up in bed.

"Like who?"

"Alicia. And she's going to bring Eddie and Oscar. They've never seen a real tennis tournament."

"What a surprise," Charlie said.

"What's that supposed to mean?"

"Nothing. Just that where they come from, people probably don't hang out on Sundays playing tennis at a fancy club."

I felt the blood rush to my face, which it always does when I get angry.

"That sounds like something Lauren would say," I snapped. "It's totally snobby, and we're not snobs. Let me remind you, Charlie, we are *not* members of the Sporty Forty. We live in the *caretaker's* cottage."

"Why do you always have to keep reminding me of that, Sammie?"

"Because it's true. You are not one of the rich kids, something you seem to be forgetting."

"They don't care if I'm rich or poor. They're my friends."

"You seem to be forgetting a recent little cheating scandal they involved you in?"

"I told you, Lauren apologized all over the place.

The other kids did, too. And I forgave them. It's like it never happened now. Everything is fine between us."

"Yeah, we'll see about that."

"You are so suspicious of everyone, Sammie. I feel sorry for you."

"Fine. In the meantime, I've invited Eddie and Oscar for tomorrow, and as far as I'm concerned, they're coming. They belong at the Sand and Surf every bit as much as Lauren or stupid Jared, who looks like he's going to trip on his shorts every time he takes a step."

Now it was Charlie's turn to snap at me. "That is his signature look!"

"Whatever." I sighed. I hated this conversation almost as much as the one I'd just had with my dad. "I'm really tired."

"Me too. Let's just go to sleep." Charlie flicked off the light and rolled over to face the wall. She didn't even say good night.

I changed clothes quickly, got into bed, and fell asleep wondering exactly when my sister had turned into such a brat.

Kicked Out

....

Chapter 6

"Miss Samantha Diamond and Miss Charlotte Diamond, last call to report to the registration desk." We could hear the official's voice over the loudspeaker even from the parking lot.

It was noon the next day and we had just arrived at the Sand and Surf Club, a few minutes later than we planned. We had been up since eight o'clock, but our dad wanted to make sure we got in a practice before we headed over for the match. Wouldn't you know it, my serve was off during practice, and my dad made me stay on the court at the Sporty Forty and do one hundred serves until I got my timing right. That didn't happen until serve number ninety-nine, and my dad wasn't pleased. In fact, he was a total crab apple. He just stood there yelling, "Ball toss! Timing! Snap your racket! Soften your grip! Watch the baseline!" and getting grumpier by the minute.

Tension on the car ride over was running pretty high. On big tournament days, my dad gets himself all in a twist, and even though this wasn't a tournament, he seemed to have put his "all in a twist" mode on high alert. He sped into the parking lot (hard to do when you have a twelve-year-old Toyota), screeched to a stop, and popped open the trunk.

"You girls get your gear and hustle in there," he said in his crab apple voice. "Be sure to apologize for being late and let them know you're ready to play immediately."

"Relax, Rick," GoGo said, giving him a gentle pat on the hand. "Nothing has begun yet. We're all fine."

"You're fine, Phyllis," he said to her. "I'm not fine with tardiness. Professional sports is like the armed forces. The trains run on time."

Okay, so the first thing I wanted to say was that nothing he said made sense. For the life of me, I didn't get how tennis had anything at all to do with trains. And the second thing was, *professional* sports? We were good tennis players, but last time I looked, no one was handing us a one hundred thousand-dollar check for our winnings. The most we'd ever won were some fake gold trophies that turned pretty rusty when we left them in the garage during a rainstorm. In my opinion, that hardly made us professional.

But he was in no mood to discuss vocabulary, so

Charlie and I just did as he said and hurried into the club. GoGo offered to stay while he parked the car. I think she was probably going to try to slow him down some. She's always such a calming force in our family, reminding us that being kind and having fun are more important than zooming around all stressed out.

The registration was taking place in the lobby at a big old mahogany desk with red velvet chairs behind it. Two stuffy-looking men were sitting in those stuffy-looking chairs, wearing stuffy-looking navy blazers with gold buttons, and striped red ties. It was weird because practically nobody in California wears jackets and ties, and certainly nobody does at a beach club.

Except those two guys. They looked us up and down and seemed tickled pink that we were wearing white tennis skirts and white tops, which is the traditional way tennis players dress. The Sand and Surf Club is so snooty, they even have a policy that all women have to wear tennis skirts and all men have to wear collared shirts—no T-shirts allowed except on the beach. I don't know where they get the idea that having a collar on your shirt makes you classy, but somehow they made that rule like three hundred years ago and it's stuck.

Charlie and I always dress alike when we play tennis because our dad thinks it's good strategy. "Makes your opponent think she's seeing double," he says. So when the man at the registration desk looked up and saw us both in white, our hair pulled back with white headbands, looking all preppy and identical, he broke into a big smile.

"What do we have here?" he said, tweaking his thin gray mustache that was clipped so short it was hardly a mustache at all. "Looks like double trouble, Ted."

"It does indeed," said the man next to him, who I'm presuming was the Ted in question. "Two little peas in a pod."

Really, Ted? Little peas? Breaking news—we're not green and round. Well, okay, maybe one of us is round. Roundish. But we're definitely not green.

"Which court are we on?" Charlie asked. She was trying to be polite, but there was a definite edge in her voice. Neither of us like it when people make a big deal out of the fact that we're twins.

"Court eleven," Mr. I-Don't-Have-Much-of-a-Mustache said. "Your match begins at exactly twelve thirty. Oh, by the way, you have three guests waiting for you on the court. They already checked in."

As we walked down the cement path to court eleven, I craned my neck to see if it was Alicia and Oscar and Eddie. Ever since last night, Charlie had been distant and cold to me, and I was hoping to see a friendly face or three.

It wasn't them, though. It was just the *opposite*— Lauren Wadsworth, Brooke Addison, and Jillian Kendall. The girls were lounging around on the bleachers, sipping iced Frappuccinos and looking ever so gorgeous in their tennis whites.

What are they wearing white for? They aren't playing.

"Charlie! Over here!" Lauren screeched, waving to Charlie as though she had been shipwrecked on a deserted island and they hadn't seen each other in twenty years.

Charlie went running up to her and all four of them hugged in that overly enthusiastic SF2 way, which is to say there was lots of squealing and jumping up and down and hand holding involved.

"Hi, Sammie," Lauren said when I strolled up and plopped my monogrammed red canvas tennis bag down on the bench. It had been a going-away gift from my mom. "Cute bag."

The one thing you have to say about Lauren is that the girl has a good eye for accessories. She never misses a new leather belt or a pair of dangly earrings. She's like one of those radar screens that lights up when she spots an expensive purse.

"Hi, Lauren," I said.

"Wasn't it so great of them to come?" Charlie said to me.

"Are you kidding?" Lauren squealed. "We wouldn't have missed it. We all came to support you guys." As she spoke, she looked behind me, her eyes searching the empty path to court eleven. "So, where's Ryan?" she asked ever so casually.

"He couldn't be here," Charlie answered. "Volleyball practice."

"Oh," Lauren said, a little frown starting to form around her mouth.

"Bummer," Jillian added.

"That sucks," Brooke noted.

"But the important thing is that we're all here together," Charlie said. "Right?"

"Right," Lauren nodded, doing a really poor job of concealing her disappointment. "So . . . do you think Ryan's coming later? Not that it matters, of course."

"He doesn't have a way to get here," Charlie said. "So I think you're stuck with just me today."

She laughed like she was making a joke, but I noticed that the other three girls didn't laugh. They just went back to their Frappuccinos and took their seats on the bleachers. Charlie and I went out on the court to warm up.

We had only been hitting a few minutes when our competition showed up. Anna Kozlov and Marjorie Shin were from the SoCal Racquet Club in San Diego. We had played them before, and they were really good. Kozlov was a hitting machine with a monster serve, and Shin was quick and fast with some of the best reflexes at the net I'd ever seen. Charlie and I ran up to say hello and shake hands with them.

"Sorry we're a little late," Anna said. "We got hung up at the registration desk."

"Yeah, there was a whole commotion going on there," Marjorie added.

"Like, what kind of commotion?" I asked, aware of an uncomfortable feeling that was taking hold in the pit of my stomach.

"There were these three kids who were trying to get into the club," Marjorie went on. "They had on totally the wrong clothes—no collared shirts and black-soled tennis shoes. Naturally, the club officials wouldn't let them in."

"I think they were from Mexico or something," Anna said. "I felt bad for them, especially for the one guy who had a messed-up foot."

That was all I needed to hear. Without a word, I raced off the court and ran at top speed down the cement path and into the lobby of the beach club where Mustache Man and his sidekick Ted were still sitting on their velvet chairs.

"Did you kick out my friends?" I demanded.

"Their attire did not meet club standards," the one called Ted answered.

"Well, I think your standards are stupid," I yelled, and before I could go on, I felt a firm hand on my arm, tugging me away from the desk. It was my dad.

"Calm down, Sammie," he said. "GoGo is with Alicia and the boys now. Everything's okay."

"Where are they?"

"I gave them some money to go get ice cream," he said. "Candido had already left, so GoGo's going to walk them down the beach to the snack bar while you and Charlie play. Everybody's happy."

"Happy? How can you say that, Dad? I'm not happy, and I'm sure they're not happy. They just got kicked out of here. I bet they were totally embarrassed and just wanted to sink into a hole and disappear."

"Sammie," my dad said, taking my face in his hands and directing my attention toward him, "you have a big match to play. Now settle down and focus. Nothing terrible happened to your friends."

"Oh, really? How would you like to get booted out by those two old stuffy dudes because you don't have a collar on your shirt? I'd say that's pretty terrible. Collars are stupid, anyway. They don't serve any purpose except to hold those stupid clothes tags, which are totally annoying."

I was yelling, and several members of the Sand and Surf Club were looking at me with raised eyebrows. I overheard one lady with a pearl necklace turn to her friend in a gold necklace and whisper, "Imagine, talking to your father like that."

"I'm going after them," I said, breaking loose from my dad's grip. "I'm not playing. I quit."

I bolted for the entrance and dashed out into the parking lot. I could see GoGo in her wide-brimmed straw hat walking with Alicia and Eddie. Oscar was trailing behind.

"Wait up, guys," I yelled and took off across the asphalt. My dad was right behind me and in about two giant steps, got in front of me and blocked my path.

"Hold it right there, young lady," he said in a stern voice. "You *are* playing today. I have committed you. Kozlov and Shin drove all the way down here from San Diego. And as your father and your coach, I will not allow you to withdraw from the match unless you are injured."

By that time, Alicia, Eddie, and Oscar had come back to where my dad and I were standing in the middle of the parking lot, staring each other down. A BMW honked at me and I stuck my tongue out at the driver. Okay, I know that wasn't mature, but it felt great. Alicia reached out and put her hand on my shoulder.

"It's okay," she said to me. "We can do something else this afternoon."

"I am so sorry," I said to her and the boys. "I invited you to come but I forgot to tell you about the dress code. And you even gave up going to Etta's party."

"I don't think they wanted us inside anyway," Eddie said.

"Everyone there has white skin and yellow hair," Oscar added.

Now it was me who wanted to drop into a hole and disappear. As if Oscar didn't have enough problems, now he had to feel bad about his skin color. Tears of anger welled up in my eyes. I wanted to say, "It's not like that, Oscar," but I knew he was right. This wasn't just about shirt collars. This was flat-out prejudice.

"Sammie and I apologize for the embarrassment we've caused you," my dad said to Oscar and Eddie and Alicia. "This whole incident was very unfortunate. But right now, Sammie needs to get on the court or she'll have to forfeit the match."

"That's fine with me," I muttered.

"It's not fine with me," he snapped back.

It was GoGo, as usual, who came to the rescue.

"Come on, kids," she said, taking Oscar's hand. "I'm dying for an ice cream. Frankie's Clam Shack on State Beach has an amazing chocolate-dipped cone." Of course, she pronounced it *cho-co-LA-tay* like they do in Spanish.

"*Me gusta el chocolate*," Oscar said. Whether he actually liked chocolate or not, I couldn't blame him for wanting to get out of the tense situation.

"Then follow me," GoGo said, turning to go. "And afterward I'll show you the tide pools. You can see mussels and hermit crabs and those cute little sea urchins."

"Can I take one home with me?" Oscar asked. "I'd like to draw it."

"Oh no," GoGo said. "On the beach, we take nothing but our time and leave nothing but our footprints."

"That's cool," Oscar said.

GoGo smiled at him and latched her arm into his.

"So is the ice cream," she said. "Wait till you taste it."

While GoGo led them away, my dad took my arm firmly and led me toward court eleven.

"I'm not playing," I said. "You can't make me."

"No, but I can ground you. And take away your allowance. And your television privileges. Need I go on?"

When we got to the court, word that Alicia and her cousins had gotten thrown out had already reached Charlie and her friends.

"OMG, aren't you so embarrassed?" Lauren said to me. "I'll bet you wanted to just die."

"Why should *I* be embarrassed?" I said. "The people at this club should be embarrassed for being total jerks."

"I think this is a really cool club," Brooke said. "My Uncle Biff is on the board here."

"Oh, is he the one who drives that classic Mercedes?" Jillian asked.

"No, that's Uncle Talbot. Uncle Biff is the one who's married to Aunt Bitsy, the one with the really huge boob implants."

I stomped away. Those girls didn't have a clue how it felt to be completely rejected. I didn't want to hear one more word about whose uncle drove which classic car. I couldn't believe that Charlie was standing there listening to them chatter on without taking a stand to defend Eddie and Oscar.

Under the threat of being grounded and stripped of all my privileges, I did play the match. I figured my dad could make me play, but he couldn't make me play well. Every time the ball came to me, I'd hit it right to Anna, who then powered up and slammed it down our throats.

"What's wrong with you?" Charlie said after we lost the first three games in a row. "You can't keep lobbing her soft balls like that. She's killing us."

"I don't care," I said.

"Well I do, Sammie. All my friends are watching. You're making me look bad."

That's just fine, I thought. Just like the people at the club had made Alicia and Oscar and Eddie look bad. I had no desire to win. All I wanted to do was leave the Sand and Surf Club and never come back again. The quickest way to do that was to lose.

Which we did. Six–love. Six–love.

That's right. We never even won one game.

You Can't
Ground Me!

....

Chapter 7

"To say I'm disappointed in you, Sammie, would be the understatement of the century," my dad fumed as we drove home after the match.

Smoke was practically coming out of his ears. He was in the middle of a long lecture that lasted all the way home and continued right on into dinner and even after. He didn't really wind down until he fell asleep on the couch watching the nightly news. Even GoGo couldn't get him to put a cork in it. He left no cliché unturned. I'm sure you can imagine the basic thrust of the lecture. Some of the highlights (which if you ask me, were actually lowlights) included:

(1) I let him and my sister down.
(2) I was part of a team.

(3) There is no "I" in team.

(4) Winners do their best at all times.

(5) Losing is for losers.

As the cherry on top of his marathon lecture, he told me I was grounded for the following week. That meant I couldn't go to any after-school activities. This was especially devastating because the Truth Tellers were going to be rehearsing every day for the performance on Saturday night. When my mom called from Boston, which she does every Sunday night to see how the week went, I told her about my punishment, hoping she would talk Dad out of it. She was very sympathetic, and agreed that what the Sand and Surf Club did was wrong, but she said she couldn't go against Dad's rules. They always back each other up, my parents, which Charlie, Ryan, and I find really annoying.

I tried calling Alicia all night, but she didn't pick up. She doesn't have a cell phone, so I just kept leaving messages on her family's voice mail. I was worried that she was mad or hurt or both, and I was desperate to talk to her—to explain, to apologize, to hear that things were okay between us.

The next morning, I left for school early and walked really fast to the bus stop at Third and Arizona, where Alicia always gets off. When the bus pulled up, she wasn't on it. I waited for the next one, but she wasn't on that one, either. Finally, I had to leave for school and found myself walking right in front of two of the SF2 boys, saggy Jared and the General.

"Hey, I hear somebody choked at her tennis match yesterday," Jared said, holding his throat and making a noise like he was choking.

Really? Don't these guys have anything better to think about than my tennis game?

Apparently not, because his remark was followed by the General's.

"Charlie says you were freaked out because your friends from Guatemala got busted," he said.

"They are from El Salvador," I said.

"Same difference," he answered.

I stopped walking and turned to look him square in the face.

"Since you seem to be a general in some unknown armed forces, you might want to take a geography lesson and learn the countries of Central America, our neighbors to the south."

"Whoa," he said, smirking at Jared. "Somebody's in a touchy mood. You should chill out and be more like your sister."

Before I could answer, his phone beeped and he reached into the pocket of his camouflage cargo pants and pulled it out.

"Text from Brooke," he said. "She's here."

We had just walked up to the front steps of Beachside, our school, and Brooke was getting out of her dad's car, holding her phone. She looked around, and when she saw the General walking toward the steps, she waved and squealed all at once. There should be a word for that ... I know, a squave. That's it. She squaved at the General.

"Hey," she said, running up to him. "How come you're walking with Sammie?"

"Are you jealous?" he asked.

"Oh right. Like, so jealous," she said with a laugh.

That stung. Not that I was interested in the General even the tiniest smidgeon of a bit, but still, it hurt not even to be considered good enough for a minute of his attention. All I was to them was a joke.

I was never so grateful to hear the five-minute warning bell ring. I left them and dashed up the stairs to the office. Mrs. Humphrey, who runs the attendance office, was in her usual foul mood, but I didn't care. I asked her if Alicia had called in sick. She just frowned at me over her steel-rimmed glasses and told me she was not at liberty to give out that information, like it was some big security breech or something.

At lunch, I went to Ms. Carew's classroom. Most of the time, she eats lunch at her desk and leaves her door open for anyone who wants to come in and hang out. The kids in Truth Tellers all love Ms. Carew, and usually, there are four or five kids in her room or on her patio, talking and eating. When I went in, she was working with Etta and Bernard, helping them refine their ideas for a monologue for our Saturday-night performance.

"Have you seen Alicia today?" I asked. "I really need to talk to her. I think she's mad at me."

"I haven't seen her," Ms. Carew answered, "but you two are such good friends, I'm sure you can talk through your feelings."

I told her what happened at the club. She listened and sighed deeply.

"Exclusion is a terrible thing," she said, "especially when you're excluded for no other reason than being yourself."

She went over to the intercom and buzzed Mrs. Humphrey.

"Can you tell me why Alicia Bermudez is out today?" she asked.

"Why does everyone want to know?" Mrs. Humphrey barked. "You'd think I have nothing else to do with my time than take attendance."

That was a weird thing to say. Since she does run the attendance office, I would think taking attendance is one of the main things she has to do. I could hear her typing on her computer, and I could feel the annoyance as she punched the keyboard hard.

"Here it is," she grumbled. "Her father called her in absent at seven forty-two this morning. He said it was a family issue."

That worried me. Was Alicia staying out of school because she was too embarrassed about what had happened at the club? Or because she was furious with me for going on with the match? Or because something bad had happened in the family? I had to talk to her. I tried calling a few more times in between classes that afternoon, but all I kept getting was voice mail.

As soon as the bell rang, I walked out the main door and headed for the bus stop at Third and Arizona. As I passed Starbucks, I saw Charlie hanging out there with Lauren, putting her backpack down on one of the outside tables.

"Sammie," Charlie called. "Where are you going?"

"I've got to do something." I stopped reluctantly at their table for just a minute. I didn't want to miss the bus.

"Um, are you forgetting that you're grounded?"

"Um, no, I'm not."

"Well, not to bother you with little details, but don't you think Dad's going to notice that you're not home like you're supposed to be?"

"Could I talk to you in private a second?" I whispered to her.

"You can say whatever you have to say in front of Lauren," she answered. "We're best friends and she'll keep any secret I ask her to. Right, Lauren?"

"Totally." Lauren nodded.

I didn't like saying anything about Alicia in front of Lauren, but I had no choice. I needed Charlie to help cover for me.

"Well, all I know is that Alicia wasn't in school today and I have to find out what's going on."

"Just call her on her cell phone and ask her," Lauren said.

"She doesn't have one."

"You've got to be kidding!" Lauren gasped. "How does a person survive without a cell phone? I know I couldn't."

"You don't think anything happened to Alicia, do you?" Charlie asked. She sounded concerned, and I was glad to hear it. Not that I wanted her to be worried, but it was good to see her acting like a real human without considering what Lauren would think.

"I don't know, I'm going to her house to check."

"What am I supposed to tell Dad?"

"Figure something out. I'll call you when I know what's happening."

As I turned to go, I nearly bumped into Brooke and the General, who were approaching the table.

"Well, look who's decided to join the human race and get a Starbucks," the General said to me. "It's about time."

Brooke laughed like he had said the cleverest thing in the world.

"Since when is drinking a Frappuccino a qualification to be in the human race?" I snapped at him.

Charlie put her hand on my shoulder and gave me a little shove.

"Just go," she whispered. "Now."

She didn't have to ask twice. I took off for the bus

stop, and luckily, the Number 86 was pulling up just as I got there. I climbed aboard and took the only seat left, next to a man in a straw cowboy hat who was sound asleep with his earbuds in. I could hear the music leaking out of them. Someone was singing in Spanish, a really lively upbeat song with lots of trumpets in the background. It was the kind of music Candido always listened to when he did the gardening at the Sporty Forty. He told me once that music and pineapple made his *corazón* happy. Of course, then he had to explain to me that *corazón* means heart in Spanish. After that, I noticed that whenever he spoke to Esperanza, he called her *mi corazón*. You have to admit, that's pretty romantic, for grown-up married people.

I transferred to the 187 bus and rode it all the way to Palms, where Alicia lives. I got off at Walpole Street and hurried down the block to her apartment. I ran up to the second floor, and knocked on the door of apartment number 206. There was a loud cry from inside, and then the door flew open. Ramon, Alicia's four-year-old brother, was standing there in his underpants and a blue cape.

"I'm Spider-Man," he screamed. "And I'm going to get you."

Then he pounced on my leg and started making buzzing noises around my ankles. Ramon's only four, so I assumed it was okay that he didn't know that bees buzz and spiders don't. I decided to pass on the science lesson.

"Ramon," Alicia's grandmother said, coming to the door. "*Basta!*"

She doesn't speak much English, but she's really nice. She beckoned for me to come in—there didn't seem to be anyone else home.

"Where's Alicia?" I asked her.

"She's been captured by Spider-Man," Ramon yelled. "He's stinging her in the butt!"

"Hey, *niño*, watch your words," said a voice from the bedroom doorway. It was Eddie, shuffling out. He looked like he had been napping. Once he was in the living room, he grabbed Ramon in his arms and wrestled him to the floor in a really playful way. Ramon giggled at the top of his lungs.

"You can tell Ramon has been around Oscar too much," Eddie said while Ramon rolled around on the floor laughing. "All he talks about now is superheroes."

"Is Alicia here?" I asked him.

"No," he said. "She's with Oscar. At the hospital."

"The hospital? Is he okay? Is she okay? I mean, is everybody okay?"

"Oscar is seeing the doctors. About his leg. They took Alicia because she speaks good English. And I got to stay here to nap!"

Of course, that made perfect sense. I started to feel some relief—maybe she wasn't as mad as I'd thought. Maybe she hadn't called because she was just busy. Still, I wanted to talk to her and make sure.

"You can wait for her here," Eddie said. I sat down

on the couch and Alicia's grandmother brought me a sugar cookie she had just baked. Ramon grabbed it and licked all the sugar off the top, then told me I could have the rest.

Call me picky, but I have a policy against eating food that has already been licked by someone else.

"No, thanks," I told him.

Eddie sat down next to me. Then he got up quickly and pulled out a piece of paper that was crunched up in the space between the cushions.

"Oscar is always leaving his drawings around," he complained.

"Can I see it?"

He handed me the sheet of paper. It was a great drawing of Captain America, his red-white-and-blue costume looking just like it did in the movie. He was running across a bridge that was on fire, carrying a blond girl in his arms. The caption under it said, "He saves Sammie from the flames."

I studied the girl in the drawing to see if she really looked like me.

"Oscar came back from your party the other night and started drawing pictures of you," Eddie said. "But he is not happy with them."

"Why?"

"He says he cannot draw a girl as pretty as you are," Eddie said.

Ramon made a sound like he was throwing up. "Eeuuwww," he gagged. "Mushy stuff makes me sick."

He continued to fake gag until I thought he actually might barf. Eddie decided it was best to change the subject, and I was all for it. The last thing I wanted was for Ramon to get any ideas about Oscar and me. Besides, nothing was going on between us anyway.

At least, I don't think anything is going on. But then, I wouldn't really know what it would feel like if something was going on. Or would I?

"Tell me about Lily," Eddie said, much to my relief.

"What do you want to know about her?"

Ramon stopped gagging and returned to buzzing around my ankle. He's usually pretty wild, or as Alicia likes to say, energetic . . . but when he's had sugar, there's no stopping him. I ignored his buzzing the best I could.

"Everything," Eddie answered.

"Well, she's more Charlie's friend than mine, so I can't tell you much about her. I know that her full name is Lily March. She modeled for the Gap catalog a couple of times. She loves to sew. Her dad is African American and he's a big-time record producer. Her mom is from Hawaii and designs bathing suits. Let's see. She's got a half-decent forehand, but no backhand whatsoever. What else do you want to know?"

"Do you think she loves me?" Eddie asked. I looked at his face to see if he was joking around. He wasn't.

"Listen, Eddie, I don't know how things work in

San Francisco Gotera," I began carefully, "but here in Santa Monica, things don't move quite that fast. We take it pretty easy on the love thing. We tend to like people for a while before we love them."

"But Lily, she told me she loves my smile," he said. "She said *loves*, not likes."

"Yeah, well, love is an expression we use a lot here in America. Like, I say I love strawberry frozen yogurt but that doesn't mean I'm *in love* with it. You understand? I think Lily was using love more in the strawberry frozen yogurt way."

"I think you are wrong, Sammie."

Maybe I was wrong. Maybe Lily had totally flipped for Eddie and was head over heels in love with him. But I felt I needed to warn Eddie against getting his feelings hurt.

"Just take things slowly," I said to him. "There are things about those kids you don't understand."

"That is just what I told Oscar today," he said. "Only I said it about you."

"About me? What could there be about me that he doesn't understand?"

"That maybe you're like those rich kids, too," Eddie said. "Maybe you pretend to like him more than you really do."

"No, I'm not like the kids at the beach club, Eddie. I say exactly what I feel and I always try to tell the truth. They play more games than I do."

"Like volleyball?"

"No. I mean yes, they do play more volleyball. But I was talking about social games. Like, who's popular and who isn't. You know, which person is the flavor of the week."

"Flavor? Are you talking about strawberry yogurt again, Sammie?"

I sighed. You don't realize how many local expressions you use until you talk to someone from another country. No wonder they say lots of stuff gets lost in translation. I heard Alicia's voice on the stairs outside, calling out to Ramon and her grandmother. She pushed open the apartment door and came in, followed by Candido. She was genuinely surprised when she saw me sitting on the couch.

"Sammie! What are you doing here?" she asked.

"I was worried."

"About what?"

"Well, it started because I couldn't reach you on the phone, and then you weren't at school and I thought you were mad about what happened at the club yesterday."

"I was mad," she said. "They were the rudest people I've ever met. But that had nothing to do with you."

"So you weren't upset that I played the match instead of coming with you guys?"

"I understood. I wouldn't want to say no to your dad, either."

"*Hola*, Sammie!" Oscar said, coming through

the apartment door a little out of breath but with a big smile on his face. It was hard work for him to climb the stairs. His left leg really couldn't handle much strain, so for him, walking up stairs was almost like having to hop the whole way.

"We have good news," he said, still breathing hard. "Tell them, Alicia."

"Well," she began, "we spent the whole day at Children's Hospital. We met with Dr. Mandel and three other doctors, too. They took X-rays and even put Oscar in a giant metal doughnut to take special pictures of his bones."

"You are taking too long," Oscar interrupted. "The good news is, the doctor can fix my leg."

"Wowee-kazowee!" Ramon cried, jumping up and down. "Then you'll be able to run really fast like the Flash!"

"I will be faster than the Flash." Oscar laughed. "I will be the fastest man alive! I will have speed force!"

He hunkered down like he was going to take off on a race, and assuming a superhero pose, extended one arm out in front of him and the other behind. But he lost his balance and toppled over on his side. Ramon didn't care. He jumped right on top of him shouting, "Speed force! Speed force!" If you ask me, it was the sugar cookie that was in full force.

"Calm down, Ramon," Alicia said. "Oscar isn't going to be fixed overnight. It's going to take a little while."

"How long?" Eddie asked.

"Well, he'll have the operation next Tuesday," Alicia explained. "He'll have to be in a cast for a while, and then do physical therapy. But soon, his leg will be normal and he won't have a clubfoot anymore."

"After all these years, my nephew will be well," Candido said. "Dr. Mandel is our angel. For all this, he charges us nothing."

There were tears in his eyes.

I felt so happy I thought my heart was going to burst. I was proud, too. Proud of my country for allowing Oscar to come here to get the medical attention he needed so badly. Proud of my city for having a wonderful place like Children's Hospital. I even felt proud of the Sporty Forty for having a member as kind and generous as Dr. Mandel.

"When my leg is better, I'm going to buy a shirt with a big collar and come to that club and play tennis with you," Oscar said, putting his arm out so I could help him up off the floor.

I reached out and took his hand and pulled him to his feet. But even after he was upright, he didn't let go. And I didn't take my hand away, either. We just stood there, holding hands.

"Tell me, Sammie," Eddie whispered. "Do you think this is strawberry frozen yogurt? Or the other thing?"

I wasn't sure what it was. The only thing I knew was that Oscar's hand was strong and warm, and it felt really nice to share that amazing moment with him.

Really nice.

The Governor

....

Chapter 8

On the bus ride home, I was so happy for Oscar that I didn't even think about what I was going to tell my dad. That changed when I got off the bus and ran (that's right, I actually *ran*) the four blocks from the bus stop to the beach club. I considered at least ten different stories about why I hadn't come home directly from school. They ranged from the very specific, such as I went to the library to research my science project on the endangered hairy-eared dwarf lemur of Madagascar, to the very weird, such as I witnessed the landing of a neon-green alien spacecraft on the beach. In the end, I decided to tough it out and go with the truth. My dad is expert at rooting out the truth, anyway.

As I approached the whitewashed fence that

borders the Sporty Forty Club, I saw two black-and-white police cars with flashing red lights in our parking lot. My mind started to race—what awful thing could have happened that required the police? I thought of that day a few months before when GoGo had gotten into a car accident and had to be rushed to the hospital. *Oh no,* I thought. *I hope everyone is okay.*

I pushed open the gate and ran inside, my heart pounding. My dad was standing on the deck talking with four uniformed officers. Charlie and Ryan were there, too. I scanned their faces anxiously to see if they looked worried. Charlie looked normal, happy actually, and Ryan was eating a banana. That was reassuring. If some terrible tragedy had occurred, he probably wouldn't just be standing there shoving a banana into his face, although knowing Ryan and his bottomless appetite, it certainly wasn't out of the question.

"Ah, here comes my other daughter, Sammie," my dad said to the officers as I slammed the gate shut. His voice turned icy. "I was expecting her some time ago."

I glanced at Charlie to try to get some idea of what she had told him.

"Esperanza leaked that you were at her house," she said with a shrug. "So I told him the truth."

"Wow, imagine that," Ryan commented, although with his mouth full of banana it sounded like "Ahmugga phat." Our mom has been telling him since forever not to talk with his mouth full. Of course, he eats constantly, so if he waited until his mouth was empty, he'd never say anything.

"I had to check on Alicia," I told my dad. "She took Oscar to the hospital."

"I hear they scheduled his operation," he said.

"How'd you know?"

"Esperanza told me that, too. I suggest, Sammie, that if you're going to break the rules, you should attempt to control your information sources more carefully."

"So we've got ourselves a little rule breaker here," one of the officers said, turning to me and sizing me up. "You better watch that, honey. You've got law enforcement on the premises, you know."

I think he meant that as a joke, but even if he did, it was a pretty marginal attempt at humor. Under the circumstances, I thought the best course of action was to change the topic entirely.

"So what's going on here?" I asked. "Did Ryan rob a bank or something?"

"You're not going to believe this," Charlie said. "The governor of California is coming here. To this very spot."

She pointed down at her feet and I noticed that her lime-green toenail polish was half chipped off. If the governor of California was coming to that very spot, my sister was going to have to get an emergency pedicure, that's for sure.

"Why is the governor coming here? Did we forget to pay our taxes?"

The other police officer, whose badge read K. BESWICK, gave out a hearty laugh.

"She's a funny one," he said to my dad. "Lots of personality."

"A little too much if you ask me," Ryan added.

"Which we didn't," Charlie and I both said in unison.

"Kids today," the first officer with the crackerjack sense of humor said. I noticed that the name on his badge read C. PORTER. "Mine squabble like that incessantly. Watch out, you three, or I'll arrest you for disturbing the peace."

Again, he said it with a straight face, but this time I could tell he was kidding when he cracked himself up after he said it.

Note to self: Police humor leaves something to be desired.

"So what's this about the governor?" I asked quickly, before he could crack another mediocre joke.

"She's attending the event here Saturday night," Officer Beswick said. "We're checking out security."

"Apparently, when Governor Corday heard about Tom Ballard's fund-raiser for the schools, she decided to make an appearance," our dad said.

"You know politicians," Officer Beswick said. "They can sniff out a photo opportunity five hundred miles away."

Wow, this was just like in the movies when the Secret Service comes to see if it's safe for the president's helicopter to land—only better. This was *for real.*

"Mind if we have a look in the house?" Officer Porter asked my dad. "I promise I won't lift anything."

He cracked up again. Wow, this guy was his own best audience.

"Not at all. Let me show you around." My dad led the way into our bungalow and both officers followed.

"Watch out for my wet suit on the bathroom floor," Ryan called after them. "You might want to wear a gas mask. It's been known to harbor some serious mold."

Once they were inside, Charlie grabbed both my hands and started to jump up and down.

"Do you know what this means?" she asked, practically bursting with joy.

"Yeah, that a really important person is coming to our house," I answered. It wasn't the most creative observation, but it did seem to answer the question.

"No, you dork!" she said. "I mean yes, but no."

"Crystal-clear thinking, as always, Charles," Ryan commented.

"You have one of those banana stringy things hanging from your lip," I pointed out, partly to silence him and partly because I think it's a family member's duty to point it out immediately when you have food on your face.

"Think about it, Sammie," Charlie went on. "You

heard Officer Beswick. What happens when Governor Corday goes someplace?"

"Um, she gives a long-winded speech and gets her pictures taken for the news."

"Bingo!" she said. "This place is going to be swarming with photographers. And you know what that means?"

"Cameras?"

"Yes! And photo opportunities galore. For me. For Lauren. For the other girls. A chance to launch our modeling careers for real. Maybe we could be discovered right here. We could even get our pictures in *Teen Vogue* magazine. Maybe even the cover! And then it's just a small step to *Seventeen* and *People*."

"Raise your hand if you've gotten totally carried away and need to be put in an insane asylum," Ryan said, walking over to Charlie and raising her arm in the air.

"Stop it, Ryan," she snapped. "You have no sense of the career opportunity this presents for a future top model."

He pretended that someone had stabbed him and, clutching his chest, fell to the ground.

"Ow. You really know how to hurt a guy," he fake moaned.

"Charlie," I said, trying to add my own touch of reality to the situation. "Don't you think the photographers are going to be here to take pictures of the governor?"

"Yes, but we'll make sure to stand close to her," Charlie said. "And you know how on the news they always film people commenting on what's going on? Well, that could be me." She cleared her voice and assumed a model-like pose, pretending to be talking to an imaginary film crew. "I am so proud to host Governor Corday at our beach club. She means everything to us," she said. "Plus, she looks great in pearls."

"I know this is a wild and crazy idea," I suggested, "but maybe you want your remarks to focus on arts education in the schools. After all, that is what the evening is all about."

"Great idea, Sammie. You can tell us all about that stuff later. Right now, I'm going to call Lauren. She is going to be so blown away."

Charlie pulled out her cell phone and flopped down on one of the chaise lounges. I could hear her chattering excitedly. Ryan went inside to inhale another armload of food, and I perched on the tabletop and looked out at the ocean, trying to process everything that had happened. My mind was churning as I watched the dark orange sun sliding down toward the horizon. It was very exciting to have the governor come to the event at the club, but not just because there would be photographers there. There would also be reporters who might stay long enough to watch our Truth Tellers performance. Maybe they would write about what we had to say. Maybe we could help raise some real money for the school arts programs.

The thought of that was so exciting, I couldn't resist. I took out my phone and called Ms. Carew to tell her the news. Her reaction surprised me. I thought she'd be all excited and screaming and everything. But instead, she got very quiet and serious.

"We have a responsibility now to be extraspecial good, Sammie," she told me. "We're not just telling the truth about ourselves, but about what having arts programs in schools means to us. Drama, dance, painting, poetry, sculpture, ceramics. We have an opportunity to represent them all to the public."

"Wow, that's a pretty big deal."

"If we raise some money so that these programs can continue to exist, that will be an even bigger deal, Sammie."

"Do you think we can do that, Ms. Carew?"

"Yes, if we work hard. We'll really dig into our rehearsals every day and try to be the best we can be."

I felt so inspired when I got off the phone. Charlie had just gotten off her call with Lauren, and she obviously felt inspired, too.

"We're all going to meet here tomorrow," she said excitedly. "The plan is to study the photos Tyler took to see which angles are best so we'll know what to do and how to pose on Saturday. It's going to be such a busy week."

"For me, too," I said.

"Why? What do you have to do?"

"The Truth Tellers are going to perform on Saturday night," I told her.

"You're kidding. They are?"

I realized she hadn't been there when Mr. Ballard had asked us, and since we barely spoke to each other on Sunday, I hadn't mentioned it to her.

"Spencer's dad asked us to," I explained.

Charlie did not seem happy with the news.

"But we want it to be a glamorous evening," she complained.

"We who, Charlie? We, as in Lauren and Brooke and Jillian?"

"There's nothing wrong with us wanting to look the best that we can. Not to insult your friends, but you know, I just can't imagine *them* on a magazine cover."

There it was again, the same conversation we'd had about Oscar and Eddie.

"Listen, Charlie, how about we do what we do, and you guys do what you do," I said impatiently.

"Please tell me you're not going to do all those weird monologues and poetry set to music."

"We speak from the heart, Charlie. We're going to speak about what having arts in the schools means to us. Hopefully that will raise some money to pay for new programs."

"Well, the first thing they should pay for is some makeovers for the art teachers. I saw that gnarly ceramics teacher, Mr. LaRue, in the cafeteria the other day. I swear, he had hunks of dried clay in his beard."

We both cracked up. As much as kids love Mr. LaRue and his ceramics program, he is known for some spectacularly bad grooming.

"What's so funny?" my dad asked, coming back outside with the officers and GoGo. I noticed the officers were eating pie-shaped slices of cheese quesadilla. Esperanza makes the best quesadillas in the world, and with GoGo's homemade salsa, it's a taste to die for. Obviously, the two of them had conspired to feed the officers.

"I think we're all set," Officer Beswick said, wiping his mouth with a napkin. "We'll coordinate with the governor's advance people and escort her limo here."

"Our officers will be posted in strategic positions," Porter said. "We'll stay until the governor is back in her car to make sure there are no incidents. You hear that, Little Miss Rule Breaker?" He fixed his eyes on me. "No incidents."

Holy cow! What is this guy thinking? That I'm going to snatch the governor's pearls and make a run for the border?

"Sammie is really very law-abiding," GoGo said. "Both my granddaughters are."

If you didn't know GoGo, you'd think she sounded all friendly, but I could hear the irritation in her voice. She didn't find Officer Porter any more amusing than I did.

"Now let me show you two gentlemen to your car," she said, holding open the gate to the parking lot. "I'm sure you have lots more preparation."

"We appreciate everything you do," my dad said to them as they made their way to the gate. "We're looking forward to Saturday. It's a real honor."

We all stood on the deck and waved good-bye, watching them climb into their police cars and drive away. After they were gone, my dad came over and gave Charlie and me a hug.

"I wish your mother were here to see this," he said. "Imagine, having the governor of California at our house."

Technically, it wasn't our house, of course. It was the Sporty Forty's house. But we did live here, and the three of us were all proud to be hosting such an important person—each for our own reasons.

"Dad," I said, taking advantage of his great mood. "I have a favor to ask."

"Sure," he said. "What is it?"

"I need to get ungrounded. I have to go to Truth Teller rehearsals this week and it's really important."

"A punishment is a punishment, Sammie," he said. Clearly, I had miscalculated how good a mood he was in.

"Rick, the kids are raising money for the schools," GoGo reminded him, ever so gently. "To support vital arts programs."

"Are you taking her side, Phyllis?" my dad snapped.

"No, I'm taking the right side," she answered,

not intimidated at all by his tone of voice. "The arts programs need money. It's as simple as that. What would life be without the arts? Just a long series of dental appointments."

Charlie was noticeably quiet. I knew she didn't want us performing Saturday night, but you'd think she could chime in with a word of support.

Nothing doing. I was on my own in this one.

"Listen, Dad," I said, going in for the kill. "If we raise enough money, Mr. Ballard said he'd even contribute some to Oscar's medical costs. The doctor and hospital are doing the surgery for free, but he's going to need money for physical therapy and crutches and stuff."

"We owe this to Esperanza," GoGo said.

"Go inside and set the table for dinner," my dad said to us, rubbing his forehead. I'm sure this was giving him a headache. "And tell Esperanza she can go home. Meanwhile, I'll consider your request."

Charlie and I ran inside the house, leaving him with GoGo. From the corner of my eye, I could see her square up to him, hands on her hips. She's little and shaped like a twig, but she's got the strength of a giant oak tree.

Charlie and I set the table in silence. There were delicious-smelling chicken quesadillas waiting for us, and a bowl of Espie's homemade guacamole, which already had a big dent in it from you-know-who-of-the-traveling-mouth. When Charlie accused

Ryan of swiping the guacamole, he denied it, but I knew better because he had green chunks in his teeth when he smiled and I can guarantee you it wasn't spinach.

"Do you think Dad's going to unground me?" I asked Charlie finally.

"Could go either way," she said.

"Fifty-fifty," Ryan agreed.

When I went out to the deck to call Dad in for dinner, he was sitting on one of the chairs, talking to GoGo. As soon as I arrived, he stopped talking.

That was either good news or bad news for me, and honestly, from the look on his face, I couldn't tell which one it was.

Dress Rehearsal

....

Chapter 9

"I have good news and bad news," my dad said, walking into the kitchen.

I hate that sentence, I really do. In my experience, the good news is never good enough to outweigh the bad news. For example, last year at my annual checkup, Dr. Hartley said, "The good news, Sammie, is you've grown two inches; the bad news is you've gained fifteen pounds."

So I think you see my point.

Anyway, I'm not going to keep you in suspense like my dad did to me. Here's what happened. He ungrounded me, sort of.

He said I was free to go to Truth Teller rehearsals after school, but there were a lot of conditions. First, I had to promise that I would play my hardest at our upcoming tournament on Sunday and never ever would I voluntarily give up a point again. I had to agree to help him and GoGo get everything set up for the party on Saturday, including cleaning the barbecue, which is a job I hate because your hands smell like barbecued chicken for a week afterward. And finally, and this was the hard part, I had to e-mail a letter of apology to the management of the Sand and Surf Club for kicking up such a fuss in the lobby.

I didn't want to agree to that condition, and I put up a big fight, but in the end GoGo convinced me to do it. After Dad went to bed, she helped me write an e-mail that was sort of an apology but wasn't totally one. It said stuff like, "I'm sorry I didn't follow your rules. Even though they seem out of date to me, I'm sure there are some of your members who think they are important." The best line was the last one, which said, "I'm sure you welcome all sorts of people to your club, and the next time my friends from El Salvador are with me, I will see that their collars are highly visible."

GoGo and I had a good laugh as I clicked SEND.

It was a busy week for both Charlie and me. She

spent a lot of time with her friends going over their pictures and rehearsing for what they were sure was their rise to stardom. I went to Truth Tellers every day after school. I wrote a monologue about how I used to be a tennis player who was only focused on winning until I discovered poetry and drama in Truth Tellers and uncovered all kinds of other emotions.

Alicia worked on a demonstration of painting techniques that people in El Salvador use for decorating handmade pottery. Will and Sara actually created a medley of different dances from the tango to the hora. They performed it while Devon read this poem:

We dance for laughter
We dance for tears
We dance for madness
We dance for fears
We dance for hopes
We dance for screams
We are the dancers
We create the dreams.

At first, a couple of us snickered when Will and Sara performed their dance routine because Will is so short and Sara is so tall. He barely comes up to her boobs. When they did the tango, you could hardly see Will. He basically disappeared into Sara's huge mane of curly hair and all you could see were his legs from the knees down. But then, Ms. Carew pointed out that the true meaning of dance is to express yourself, and not just to look good for other people. We all said we were sorry and applauded like crazy when they did their dance again.

The dress rehearsal was on Friday. Alicia asked if she could bring Oscar and Eddie to see it. Oscar was starting to get nervous about his operation, and she felt coming to Truth Tellers would be a good distraction. Besides, he had been nagging her all week about wanting to see me. This was the only chance he'd get, though, because I was still officially grounded after five p.m. and had to hurry home right after Truth Tellers.

We took a vote, and it was a unanimous yes. Oscar and Eddie could come.

On Friday, a couple of the moms and dads came to be in our test audience, too, as well as Bernard's sister Veronica and Keisha's cousin Brandon. I asked Charlie to come, but she was having a final meeting with her top-model group to rehearse important-sounding things to say about the arts. Spencer's dad had told them their chances of getting on TV were best if they had short, quick, punchy things to say to the camera. "Sound bites," he called them. Charlie was trying to decide if hers should be "Art is smart" or "Art in school will help us rule." You should have heard Jillian's sound bite. She planned to say that studying painting in school helped her learn how to apply eyeliner.

Yes, it's true, and may I also add, it's the deepest thought Jillian Kendall has ever had!

After school on Friday, Alicia and I waited on the front steps to meet Oscar and Eddie. I hadn't seen Oscar all week, and I was looking forward to seeing him. I guess you could call it looking forward. I felt like I had butterflies in my stomach, like the way you feel when you're waiting in line before you go on a roller coaster. Kind of excited and nervous and afraid all at the same time.

"Are you nervous about the performance?" Alicia asked me.

"No, not really."

"Well, you seem nervous, Sammie. Anything I can do?"

"I'm feeling kind of weird," I said.

"Like you're getting the flu? That would be horrible on the day before the event."

"No, physically I'm fine. I just keep thinking about . . ." I hesitated. Alicia was my best friend. I could tell her anything. I took a breath and plunged in. "I just keep thinking about Oscar."

Alicia nodded.

"I think about him, too," she said. "It's a big operation he's going to have. I just pray everything comes out okay and nothing goes wrong. He's very special to me."

"To me, too," I whispered, before I could stop myself. "When I first met him, I thought he was sweet. But now I'm thinking about him more and more in a different kind of way."

Alicia held up her hand to stop me from going on.

"Listen, Sammie," she interrupted. "Oscar is my cousin. My family is here to protect him. None of us want him hurt."

"I would never hurt him, Alicia."

"I know you wouldn't intentionally. But you don't know how he feels about you."

"Do you?"

"No, not exactly. But I can see he likes you, in a special way. And right now, he should be only concentrating on one thing—getting through the surgery and recovering fully. That's what we all want for him. I'm sure that's what you want for him, too."

"Yes, of course I do."

"Then let him be," she said. "Nothing can get in the way of this operation."

Before I could ask her what she meant, Candido pulled up in his truck. I followed Alicia as she ran over and flung open the door. Oscar and Eddie climbed out, all dressed up, with pressed white shirts (wouldn't you know it, *with* collars!) and their hair slicked back like they were going to Sunday school.

"You guys look great," I said, being careful to include both of them and not just talk to Oscar.

"We don't want to embarrass you again," Oscar answered, and I wanted to cry.

We walked into the main building. I walked slowly so that Oscar could keep up. It was *me* who didn't want to embarrass *him*.

We headed down the hall but stopped when we saw Charlie at her locker. She was standing there talking with Lauren, Lily, and Jillian.

"Eddie," Lauren called out, waving at him as if Alicia, Oscar, and I were totally invisible.

Eddie's face lit up when he saw Lily and he veered over to them so fast he practically left skid marks on the linoleum floor.

"Eddie, we need to get to Ms. Carew's class," I said. "You're part of the audience and it's showtime."

"Actually, Eddie," Lily said, "I was just thinking that maybe you want to come back to the Sporty Forty with us." She flashed him a really inviting smile.

"Yeah," Jillian agreed, getting into the flirt fest. "It'd be a shame for all your fancy clothes to go to waste."

Okay, I'm not even going to deal with the fact that she had reduced our whole Truth Tellers performance to being a "waste." Jillian couldn't help it if her idea of a peak meaningful experience was watching the *Real Teen Makeover* marathon on reality TV. But I did object to the fact that we had invited the boys to our event and now the SF2s were trying to mess that up.

"Thanks," I said, speaking for Oscar and Eddie, "but they want to come see what we're doing."

Eddie looked at Lily and I could practically see hearts boinging out of his eyes, like you see on cartoons when the characters fall in love.

"I would like to go to the beach club," Eddie said, directing his answer to Lily. No surprise there.

"I'll stay with you, Sammie," Oscar said, which was a good thing, because he hadn't even been invited to go with them.

"Then it's settled," Charlie said, slamming her locker shut. "We can all meet up later."

"Oh, look, there's Ryan," Lauren said. "Ryan, over here!"

Ryan was walking down the hall with Ben Feldman and a bunch of his other volleyball team friends. They are the tallest people in the school, so they stand out like a bunch of flagpoles. Lauren waved to him and tossed her gorgeous hair over her shoulder in that bouncy way she does. Too bad the gesture was lost on our doofus brother. He just gave Lauren a wave and called out, "Hey, dudettes, looking good!"

"We're on our way to the club," she called out. "Eddie's coming. Want to come?"

"Nah, that guy's way too good-looking," Ryan

called back. "I can't compete with him."

This did not sit well with Lauren, who is used to getting her way all the time. But she didn't want to appear to beg in front of her girlfriends (she has to protect her queen-bee status), so she just locked her arm in Charlie's and said, "Let's go. He doesn't know what he's missing."

"I'll catch up with you guys after practice," Ben called out. "Hold a place for me."

Just like that, Lauren and the girls left, and in two seconds, Alicia, Oscar, and I were a threesome. That seemed to be the way it was going to be.

When we got to Ms. Carew's room, Oscar sat with the parents. He really seemed to enjoy the performance. He bounced his head to Bernard's drumbeat, clapped his hands during the dance routine, and listened carefully as I spoke about how the arts were changing my life. When the performance was over, he waited for me while Ms. Carew gave me my final notes. She wanted to talk with Alicia a little more, so Oscar and I headed out to the truck to tell Candido it'd be a few more minutes. He carried my backpack as we left the room and headed down the hall.

"I liked what you did, Sammie, but what I really enjoyed was the dancing," he told me as we walked. "As soon as I get my leg fixed, I am going to learn to dance. I love music, but I look funny dancing."

"You're going to be a great dancer, Oscar. I bet you're going to burn up the dance floor."

"Ah, like the Human Torch," he said. "His whole body can explode in flames."

"Whoa there." I grinned. "I didn't mean you'd actually set fire to anything. I just meant that every girl in San Francisco is going to line up to dance with you." I mentioned the other girls on purpose. Alicia's words were still ringing in my ears, and I was trying not to give Oscar the impression that I was his girlfriend or liked him in any special way.

"I'm sure there are lots of girls in your town who have huge crushes on you," I went on.

He just laughed, and all I could think about was what a great smile he had. Before I knew it, he took my hand and twirled me around.

I spun under his arm, and when I came back around to face him, the smile was gone and his face was close to mine. It occurred to me that he might kiss me, right there in the hall in front of the attendance office!

I held my breath.

But he didn't kiss me. Instead, he threw his other arm high in the air, tossed his head back and shouted "Human Torch, flame on!"

I burst out laughing, partly because it was funny and partly because I was relieved. If he had kissed me, I don't actually know what I would have done. I've never had a real kiss before.

"No, Sammie. Nobody laughs at the Human

Torch," he said, a little hurt. "Of all the superheroes, he is my favorite."

"I'm sorry, Oscar," I said. "It's just that no one has ever said 'flame on' to me before."

"Then you are missing a lot, *mi corazón.*"

Wait. Did he actually call me that? Yes, he did. Was he being funny or was he being serious? I wish I understood Spanish. Or boys. Or both.

As we headed out to Candido's truck, I kept thinking about how much Oscar loved superheroes. At the exact moment when I felt like he was going to speak from his heart, instead he spoke in the voice of a superhero. I understood that. For him, superheroes were something much more than entertainment. He loved those guys so much—they were with him all the time, in his heart and his imagination. He even wanted to create new ones when he grew up. He spoke through them, felt powerful through them. If I were disabled and had trouble just walking, I would love superheroes, too. I would dream of being able to fly, or burst into flames, or have powers that would make me strong and mighty.

Oscar had picked the strong and mighty as his best friends. So what if they weren't real?

When Alicia arrived, we all climbed into Candido's truck and drove to the club so he could drop me off and pick up Eddie. When we pulled up in front, I said a quick good-bye to Oscar and jumped out to tell Eddie it was time to go. I pushed open the gate, and inside the usual things were going on. Jillian, Brooke, and Lauren were sitting at one of the beach tables, looking at old issues of *People* and *Us Weekly* magazines. The boys were playing beach volleyball, and Lily and Charlie were out there with them. Lily was on the same team as Eddie, and Charlie was on the same team as Spencer. My dad must have been giving a tennis lesson on the courts, or he would have been out there shouting at Charlie not to injure herself before the tournament.

But the amazing thing was Eddie. He was on the beach in the middle of the game, laughing and high-fiving and fist-pumping with the guys like he had been one of the SF2s all his life. Even Jared and Sean were acting like he was their new best friend. Since when had he become the flavor of the day?

"Hey, Eddie, Candido's waiting for you in the truck," I called, walking out onto the sand.

"Oh, don't go yet," Lily begged.

"He has to," I answered a little too sharply. I don't know why I resented the fact that Eddie had become such an instant SF2 favorite. He had a right to make friends. Still, my heart was with Oscar, who was sitting out in the truck with only his uncle and cousin for company. He had the same sweet personality as Eddie, the same handsome face, the same kind heart. He just happened to get a bum leg. It wasn't fair.

"I'll go tell Candido that we want you to stay,"

Jared said to Eddie. "He'll say yes. After all, the guy works for us. He says no and he's fired."

That did it. I lost it.

"Candido doesn't work for you," I barked. "He works for the whole club. You can't fire him, Jared. And just because your parents have enough money to pay dues here doesn't give you the right to act like a big shot when you're not."

"Whoa there, Sammie," Sean said. "Take it down a notch before you start foaming at the mouth."

I felt my hand form into a fist, and I swear I would have popped him one if Spencer hadn't spoken up.

"Take it down a notch yourself, buddy," Spencer said to Sean. "Candido is a great guy, and it's not up to us to boss him around."

Charlie dashed over to me and put her hand on my shoulder.

"Calm down," she whispered. "All they're saying is that they like Eddie and want him to stay."

The attention must have embarrassed Eddie, because he had left the volleyball court and was over on the deck putting on his shoes.

"Where are you going?" Lily asked him.

"My brother is waiting for me," he said.

I wanted to reach out and hug him. By the way, I think Lily did, too, but not for the same reason.

The guys came over and crowded around him, giving him fist pumps and playful slugs and "later dudes" and a variety of other boy-type good-byes.

"You're coming to my dad's thing tomorrow night, right?" Spencer asked him.

"Can Oscar come, too?" he asked.

"Of course he can," I stated, before anyone else had a chance to jump in. "We want both Oscar and Eddie, don't we, guys?"

I glared at Charlie, who looked a little uncomfortable.

"Don't we, Charlie?" I repeated.

She looked over at Lauren and Jillian and Brooke, who were all staring at her, waiting for her answer. They did not look happy.

"Sure," Spencer piped up. "Everybody's welcome."

I continued to glare at Charlie, amazed that she had let Spencer answer for her.

This was not the sister I knew.

The Big Night

Chapter 10

"Sammie, move the lanterns a couple feet to your left," my dad instructed. "The governor will not thank us if we leave her standing in the dark when she makes her speech."

We were stringing orange-and-white Japanese-style paper lanterns across the deck.

"Why can't Ryan do this?" I grumbled. "He's so tall, he wouldn't even need a ladder. My arms are twitching from holding them up so high."

"Remember that feeling next time you decide to purposely lose a match," my dad said.

That's my dad. He just can't resist any opportunity for a lecture.

I had been working all day to get the club ready for the fund-raiser, and I felt like Cinderella before the ball. Charlie and her pals (who I began to think of as the wicked stepsisters) had done nothing to help—unless you consider trying on a million different outfits helpful, which personally, I don't.

Because I was technically still being punished, I had to do all the grunt work. I swept the deck so it was free of all sand, cleaned the barbecue, put out checkered tablecloths and napkins, helped GoGo cut up chicken for skewers, and took a few already cooked ones and a plate of brownies to Mrs. Ivanov next door. She's an elderly retired Russian ballet dancer who lives alone in the old, brown shingle house next to our club. GoGo says Mrs. Ivanov's husband bought her that house over fifty years ago, when she was young and beautiful and an international ballet star. Now her husband is gone and she is old and weak, so GoGo likes to send over meals to her whenever she can.

By the time we finished stringing the lights, it was five o'clock, almost time for the party to start. I had just enough time to jump in the shower and change clothes. Even though I was in a hurry, I "pulled a Charlie" and tried on about six outfits before I made my final decision. Now Charlie, she tries things on to see what looks best. Me, I try things on to see what fits. That night, the zipper of my favorite jeans decided to get all temperamental and uncooperative. It refused to zip up, no matter how much I held my breath and sucked my stomach in. I'm sure you'll agree with me when I say it had absolutely nothing to do with the fact that I polished off all of Charlie's french fries the night before.

Hey, I wanted to wear the bigger-size jeans, anyway. (Not.)

I picked out a navy shirt that was long enough to cover the roll of fat that pooched out over the top of my too-tight jeans. Ryan calls this particular area of my body a "muffin top," which sounds a whole lot cuter than it actually is. Without looking in the mirror, I smoothed my hair and hurried outside where I found Charlie and Ryan already waiting at the gate for Lauren and the other girls to arrive. Unlike me, Charlie was wearing her size-minus-zero jeans and a short little T-shirt. Not a muffin top to be found. She had a lip gloss wedged in her pocket and kept taking it out and nervously applying layer after layer.

"Your lips are getting pretty goopy," I said.

"They were supposed to be here at six."

"Who was? Your lips? They're already here."

"Very funny, Sammie. That sounds like something Ryan would say."

She had a point. I was nervous about having to perform at the event, nervous about seeing Oscar again, and I have a tendency to make bad jokes when I'm uncomfortable.

"Hey, I resent that remark," Ryan said. "My humor is high quality. For example, pull my finger."

He held his index finger straight out in front of us,

and when we both refused to pull it, he did it himself, then made a farting sound and burst out laughing.

"I need a ginger ale after that," he said, and sauntered off, still chuckling.

"Just shoot me if I ever behave like that," I said to Charlie, but she wasn't listening. She pulled out her lip gloss again and said, "I wonder what's keeping them." It was like I wasn't even there.

Charlie was really disappointed when the first people to arrive were Oscar and Alicia. Eddie had spent the afternoon swimming at Lily's house, and since her dad was dropping them off, Candido only had to bring Oscar and Alicia. They climbed out of Candido's truck, and Alicia stood at the open door for a long time, making arrangements about when to get picked up.

"Look who came with me," Oscar said as he limped up the path. He turned to show me the back of his gray hoodie. It said THE HUMAN TORCH in bright orange letters surrounded by yellow flames.

"That's very hot," I said, making my second lame joke of the evening. All I could do was hope this wasn't a trend and that I could stop at two.

Alicia breezed right by us into the kitchen to unwrap the El Salvadorian pottery she had brought to use in her demonstration. Candido drove off just in time to make room for a black Mercedes station wagon to pull into the driveway. Of course, it belonged to Lauren's dad, Chip Wadsworth.

"I'm going to let the girls off here while I go park in the lot," Mr. Wadsworth called out to us. "Apparently, the walk from the parking lot will ruin their hair."

Lauren shot her dad a look and then got out of the car with Jillian and Brooke.

All three girls walked up to the gate, and I swear, you've never seen such hair-bouncing in your life. It was like they were walking in slow motion. I don't know what they used to get their hair so thick and springy, but they looked like they had stepped right out of a shampoo commercial. Bounce, step, bounce, step, bounce, step. Even Oscar couldn't take his eyes off them—that is, until Tyler Frank came careening in, his silver sports car pulling to a stop in front of us.

"It's the Batmobile!" Oscar exclaimed, his attention immediately turning from the girls to the Ferrari.

"Bruce Wayne, reporting for duty." Tyler did a little salute as he hopped out of the car. "How are things in Gotham?"

"Huh? We don't live in Gotham," Lauren answered, looking confused.

"It's a little joke," Tyler explained, giving Oscar a friendly punch. "For us Batman fans."

"Oh," Lauren said. Then she laughed as though she had gotten the joke in the first place. She stopped just as suddenly as she started, changing the topic to what she really wanted to talk about.

"So, Tyler, we're all ready for you to make us stars."

"How do you figure?" he asked. "I'm supposed to be covering the governor."

"Just wait and see," Lauren told him. "Wherever she is, we won't be far away. Isn't that right, models?"

Jillian and Brooke nodded vigorously, and so did Charlie. In fact, her head was wagging up and down so much she looked like one of those bobblehead dolls.

"Would it be okay if I sat in your car?" Oscar asked Tyler. "I won't touch anything, I'll just take a look around."

"Later, dude," Tyler said. "I've got to unload my camera gear and get set up now. You can check out the car when things settle down. In the meantime, I'd like to get a couple shots of you inside the club."

"You want to photograph *him*?" Lauren asked incredulously. "Why?"

"You kidding? He's got a great face," Tyler said. "And a great story. Plus, any pal of the Human Torch is a pal of mine."

Tyler handed Oscar one of his camera bags to carry. Oscar slung it over his shoulder, which already was supporting his own goofy-looking bright-red backpack, and headed off into the club. The heavy load made him limp even more than usual. Tyler grabbed another equipment bag and a tripod from the trunk and followed Oscar in. The pack of future models trailed close behind him. No surprise there, I guess. They couldn't wait to get their faces in front of his lens.

I was relieved to see them all go. That left Alicia and me by ourselves to greet the other Truth Tellers who were starting to pull up. Ms. Carew arrived with Sara and Will in her car. Etta, Devon, and Bernard were all dropped off by their parents. None of their parents were going to stay for the performance, though. Since it was a fund-raiser, everyone was supposed to pay money to come in. The suggested donation, which was more like a command than a suggestion, was two hundred and fifty dollars per person. That wasn't a problem for the members of the Sporty Forty, but the parents of my friends didn't have that kind of money to throw around. Not that contributing to a good cause is throwing around money—it's just that my friends' parents' money went to pay for necessities, like food and rent and clothes.

The first guests to arrive were Dr. Mandel, his wife, and their son, Noah. Noah is in the same grade as Ryan, but they don't exactly hang out together. Noah is this amazing science genius who's whipped through all the high school science electives even though he's only in the eighth grade. Let's just say, my brother's interest in science is limited to why humans fart and burp.

"You're one of the twins," Noah said to me as they stopped at the gate.

"Sammie Diamond," I replied, holding out my hand.

He didn't take it. He just said, "I suppose you

know what the incidence of monozygotic twins is worldwide."

There was an awkward silence while I waited for him to answer. He didn't.

"Um...what exactly is a monozygotic twin again?" I asked. "I used to know, but suddenly it's just slipped my mind."

"It's you," he said. "Identical. Formed from the same genetic material."

Okay, so I feel marginally idiotic.

I quickly turned to face Dr. Mandel to cover my embarrassment.

"Thank you so much for what you're doing for Oscar," I said, changing the subject to something I did know about. He looked surprised.

"Oh, is he a friend of yours?"

"Yes," I said. "His cousin Alicia is my best friend."

"Ah, yes, Candido's daughter." Mrs. Mandel nodded. "All the Sporty Forties are so fond of Candido. I'm sure his nephew is a deserving young man."

"He'd better be," Dr. Mandel commented. "His surgery is costing the hospital well over fifty thousand dollars. Good thing Candido has friends in high places."

"Oscar's inside, if you'd like to say hi," I said. "He's wearing a Human Torch sweatshirt. You can't miss him!"

"My dear girl," Dr. Mandel said. "Not only do I know what Oscar looks like, I know what his bones look like. Don't forget, I have examined his X-rays."

"Of course," I said, feeling idiotic for the second time in ten seconds, a new world record even for me.

Note to self: When talking to smart people, try not to be such a moron.

I followed the Mandels as they entered the club. When they went to go get drinks, I heard Noah explaining to his parents the science behind how the Human Torch's body produced his fire powers.

All the Truth Tellers had arrived and I was the last one to join the group. We huddled with Ms. Carew to scope out the best place for our performance. We decided to make a little stage at the end of the deck facing away from the beach, under the paper lanterns. We dragged three potted palm trees into a semicircle to create a performance area. Ms. Carew had borrowed a portable mic from school and we placed that in the center. Bernard, who considers himself a major techie, plugged it in. Not all that technical, if you ask me, but he made a big deal out of it because it required . . . hold on to your seats . . . an extension cord!

When Oscar was finished getting his pictures taken by Tyler, we let him do the sound check. He hummed a few bars of the Batman theme into the mic and got such a huge kick out of it, he did it again, even louder this time. From across the deck where she was standing with Lauren, Charlie shot me a nasty glance, shook her head, and mouthed the words, "That's not happening."

As much to protect Oscar as to help Charlie,

I went over and pulled the microphone plug from the extension cord. Charlie flashed me a silent nod of approval.

A few minutes before the rest of the guests were set to arrive, Officers Porter and Beswick showed up in their police cars, each with one additional officer. After doing a quick check of the premises, the two new officers stationed themselves in the clubhouse, next to an extra tray of brownies. Officer Beswick manned the front gate of the club, while Officer Porter walked around the beach eyeing everyone up and down. I saw him stop and talk with Oscar, which I thought was strange, because he didn't stop and talk to anyone else. After that, he took out his walkie-talkie and said something to Officer Beswick.

Mr. Ballard and Spencer arrived at exactly six thirty. I went over to say hello and tell the councilman that the Truth Tellers were very excited about performing. While I was talking, I noticed Spencer slip away and quickly go to join Charlie and the girls. He didn't do it in a mean kind of way, just in an "I'm here to see your sister" no-nonsense kind of way. I didn't hold it against him. As for Mr. Ballard, he quickly switched the conversation from Truth Tellers to the rest of the evening's plans. I admired how smoothly he did it. I guess politicians are used to making the conversation go the way they want it to.

"We're planning on about one hundred people showing up," he said to my dad and GoGo. "Before we start the program, let's give folks an hour to mingle and enjoy this young lady's delicious finger food."

He put his hand on GoGo's shoulder to make it clear that she was the young lady in question. My dad laughed.

"What's so funny, Rick?" GoGo said to him. "I am definitely young in spirit."

"That's the attitude," Mr. Ballard said, slapping GoGo on the back with such enthusiasm it almost knocked her over. Then he got all serious again.

"After the mix and mingle, I'll introduce the governor. She's on a tight schedule, but her advance people tell me she should be here by seven thirty, hopefully in time to see the Truth Teller kids perform."

I love the sound of that! The governor of California, watching us do our thing. Wow.

"Afterward, I imagine she'll want to say a few words about helping the schools and so on and so forth, pose for the usual photos, hopefully a few with yours truly, and we'll have her on her way by eight. How's that sound?"

"Totally amazing," I said, even though no one had asked me.

Mr. Ballard laughed his big laugh and slapped me on the back, too. I was prepared, though, and remained upright.

"All right, folks," he said. "Let's get this show on the road, shall we?"

From that moment on, everything went into fast motion. It was astonishing to see how quickly the beach club filled up. One minute it was practically empty, and by six forty-five, the deck was swarming with well-dressed people sipping drinks and chatting away. Most of the members brought their kids. Sean and Jared were there, looking bored and superior. The Feldmans were there but without Ben. They said he was sleeping over at his cousin's birthday party in Disneyland. That sounded pretty awesome. The General did show up, wearing a shirt and tie and dressy pants. It was actually the first time I had ever seen him out of his camouflage uniform.

"So I guess since you're a civilian tonight, I don't have to salute," I said to him as he got a Coke from the bar.

"Is that supposed to be funny?" he asked.

Okay, I admit it wasn't hilarious. But it wouldn't have killed him to just laugh a little and then take a swig of his Coke. He didn't have to be such a jerk about it.

I guess when you're a jerk, it's hard not to be a jerk. That's all there is to it.

The General went to join Sean and Jared, and they stood around looking bored together. I wondered if their parents had paid two hundred and fifty dollars each for them to come. I couldn't imagine what it would be like to have so much money that you could spend two hundred and fifty dollars to bore the pants off your kids.

The SF2 girls were the opposite of bored. Led by Lauren, they followed Tyler around like a herd of high-heeled sheep as he shot pictures of the well-dressed crowd. They plastered on smiles and stuck their heads into every group shot. I was surprised to see how aggressive Charlie was in the sticking-her-head-in-the-shot game. I remember when she was a shy little kid who would hide behind me when GoGo would take us to the mall to get our picture taken with Santa Claus. Now here she was, mugging at the camera and sticking her face in every time a flash went off.

By seven thirty, it was almost dark and the governor still hadn't arrived. Mr. Ballard checked his watch nervously.

"I don't want folks to go home," he told Ms. Carew, "so I think we had better get on with the show. The governor must be stuck in traffic."

Ms. Carew gathered up all the Truth Tellers for a last-minute pep talk.

"I don't want to start yet," Bernard complained. "I want to wait for the governor."

"Me too," Will agreed. "I was planning to ask her to dance after Sara and I finish our routine."

"We don't have a choice about when we go on," Ms. Carew said. "We're performing at the request of Councilman Ballard, and he's asked us to begin.

So begin we shall. Sammie, I'd like you to go first. Your monologue is a very appropriate way to kick things off."

My heart leaped into my throat. I wished she had asked someone else to go first. I was the newest member of Truth Tellers and the most inexperienced.

"But, Ms. Carew—" I began.

"Just do your best out there," she said before I had a chance to protest. "Be honest when you speak, and concentrate on what you're feeling. Speak from the heart. All the rest will follow."

Alicia took my hand as we prepared to go onstage. Both our palms were a sweaty mess. I looked out into the crowd and got even more nervous, if that was possible. It wasn't easy performing in front of so many people. Especially this group of fancy, rich people.

"I don't see Oscar," I said.

I scanned the horizon and could barely make out the group of SF2 boys down on the beach. They looked like purple shadows against the night sky. I saw Eddie with them, but I didn't think Oscar was there. "I don't see him down there with the other guys," I said.

"It's just like them, isn't it?" Alicia said. "They can't even be part of the audience. I'm sure they consider us too boring to watch."

I really wished I could find Oscar in the crowd. Even though I was nervous, I wanted him to see me perform. I thought I was going to faint when Mr. Ballard walked up to our little stage and tapped on the microphone to get everyone's attention.

"I can't do this," I whispered to Alicia.

"Yes, you can, Sammie. Just believe in yourself."

"Welcome, ladies and gentlemen," Mr. Ballard began in his big, booming voice. Miraculously, the glasses stopped tinkling and the crowd grew silent.

"I thank you for coming out tonight to raise money for this worthy cause," he said. "We want our kids in America to be exposed to all the arts ... music, drama, drawing. In fact, you know what they call an American drawing, don't you? A Yankee doodle!"

Only a few people chuckled, but it didn't matter to Mr. Ballard. He laughed like he was being tickled under his arms.

"We're hoping Governor Corday will join us tonight, but while we're waiting, I want to introduce you to a great bunch of kids. They call themselves the Truth Tellers, and they're here to show us what participating in an arts program can do. Kids, the stage is all yours."

We filed onto the stage and Ms. Carew introduced us one by one. Then it was my turn to go on. As I walked up to the microphone, I was sure I could hear my knees knocking against each other. I was doing that nervous sweating thing I do, and I could feel little beads of perspiration forming on my upper lip.

Stay calm, I told myself. *Ignore the sweat spurting from your face. Speak from the heart. The rest will take care of itself.*

I took a deep breath and began.

"My name is Sammie Diamond," I said, "and before I found Truth Tellers, I was a jock. What mattered to me was winning. But then I discovered—"

Before I could say another word, I heard the sound of a siren approaching the club. A police car, its lights flashing, pulled up to the gate, and behind it, a big black limousine. Everyone turned away from the stage. Officer Beswick sprang into action, shining his flashlight onto the limo. The windows were blacked out and we couldn't see inside. Then the door opened and a tall woman with perfectly styled blond hair and wearing a red suit stepped out. As if by magic, Tyler Frank was suddenly next to her, snapping pictures as she made her way into the crowd. Charlie and Lauren and their crew surrounded her, sticking their heads into the shot and waving and smiling.

Governor Corday ignored all the fuss and made her way directly up to the stage.

"Hello, Tom," she said to Mr. Ballard. "Glad I could make it. What do we have here?"

"A presentation by the Truth Tellers, Governor," he said. "Some of our fine kids who are involved in the arts."

Governor Corday smiled. She looked picture-perfect, every hair in place.

"Very good," she said. "I'm eager to hear what they have to say."

Brushing aside the photographers, she took a seat in the front row. She looked right at me, adjusted her pearls, nodded, and waited for me to begin. The governor of the whole state . . . and her pearls . . . were waiting for me.

Take that, Lauren Wadsworth! Take that, size-minus-zero jeans! Take that, bouncy-haired top models! Take that, my sweaty upper lip!

Look at me and watch where the truth can take you!

Flame On!

....

Chapter 11

"Drama. Dance. Art. Poetry," I heard myself saying at the end of my talk. "These are the ways we humans express our deepest truths. These are the ways we ask questions and seek answers. All forms of art bring us beauty and joy. When I was only an athlete, winning was the answer. Now that I am an artist, it is the questions that matter. The questions that allow me to find my path and find the truth about who I truly am."

Everyone in the audience had stopped talking and munching on appetizers and stood still, listening to what I, Sammie Diamond, had to say. As I ended my speech and moved away from the microphone, my ears filled with the sound of applause. It wasn't just polite applause, either. It felt real. Councilman Ballard let out a loud whoop. Lily March's mom yelled, "That's telling it like it is, Sammie!" Even the governor gave me a standing ovation. I was dizzy with excitement. All I could focus on was her shiny scarlet nails creating a moving red blur as she applauded.

I wasn't the only one who got a standing ovation. The rest of the Truth Tellers were amazing, too. And when Will and Sara ended the program with their dance medley, the crowd went nuts. Will was so happy, he must have taken fifteen bows. I'm telling you, he looked about six feet tall.

"These young people have done a truly outstanding job," Governor Corday said to the crowd when we finished our presentation. "They're a fine example of why we need to support the arts in our schools. Bravo, Truth Tellers!"

She stood on our little stage, clapping her hands in honor of us. Well, she was clapping the best she could because the wind had really kicked up during our performance and was blowing her perfect hair so it was sticking straight up from her scalp. In between claps, she'd reach up to try to smooth it down, very aware that Tyler was clicking away on his camera. I'm no expert at politics, but I'm pretty sure the last thing a governor wants is to have her picture taken when she looks like she just stuck her finger in an electrical socket.

Will was determined to dance with the governor. When she finished her remarks, he actually asked her to dance, although with the wind whirling around her ears, I'm not sure she heard him. He took that as a yes. Before she could ask him to repeat himself, he put his arm around her waist, and I swear this is true, actually laid his head somewhere on her chestal area. From my vantage point, I couldn't see exactly where it landed, but it was definitely above the waist and below the pearls. Will wasn't trying to be inappropriate or anything, it just so happened that because he's short, his head could only reach that delicate part of her anatomy.

Governor Corday was classy enough to laugh it off and let Will take her on a spin, but when he tried to dip her, she was way too heavy for him and started to sink to the ground. In a show of great reflexes, Spencer leaped up from the audience to catch her before she hit the deck. Simultaneously, Ms. Carew reached out and grabbed her hand. Between the two of them, they saved her from landing smack on her behind. Recovering her composure immediately, the governor shook Ms. Carew's hand like she had always planned to do it and Tyler snapped some more pictures. It was a totally impressive recovery.

Governor Corday went all the way down the line and shook each of our hands while she delivered a personal compliment. She told Alicia that the pottery decorations she demonstrated were beautiful and should never become a lost art. She told Bernard he was quite the drummer. You'll notice that her comment carefully avoided the question of whether or not he's a *good* drummer. She told Sara and Will that they should consider trying out for a dance reality show on TV. All the while, Tyler was snapping pictures like a madman.

When the governor got to me, she pressed my hand warmly and told me how brave I was to reveal my vulnerability in a public forum. She said she wished more politicians would learn from that example. Then she stood right next to me so Tyler could get a shot of just the two of us. I looked out and saw Charlie and Lauren and the other girls watching me get a solo picture taken with the governor. At first, it felt great. Then it felt bad. Then it felt great again. Then it felt great and bad at the same time. The truth is, I couldn't totally enjoy the moment because I was getting what they wanted so badly.

I know what you're thinking, and I'm thinking the same thing. Should I or shouldn't I?

I'll cut to the chase here. I decided I should. For Charlie. For our family. For GoGo, who always says, "When you have a choice between taking the high road and taking the low road, go high."

"Governor Corday, I have a favor to ask of you," I blurted out.

"What is it, Sammie?"

Did she say Sammie? Yes, she did. Wow, she remembers my name. Could this night possibly get any better?

"Would you mind taking one more picture, with my sister and her friends?" I asked.

"Oh, are they Truth Tellers, too?"

"No, no, no," I said with a laugh. "They're so totally not Truth Tellers."

She raised an eyebrow and I realized how bad that sounded. "Well, not that they're liars," I sputtered, "but they're not technically Truth Tellers. I mean, they're not officially in our group, but they have their own group, and they'd really like to get their picture taken with you."

I hoped she wasn't going to ask what their group was, because saying they wanted to be models and have their faces plastered on the cover of *People* magazine didn't have a great ring to it.

"Of course, ask them to come up right away." Then she whispered in my ear. "Tell them to hurry before this wind blows my wig right off."

"That's a wig?" I whispered back, stunned that she would just out-and-out say it.

"I don't share that information with everyone, Sammie, but you're a Truth Teller. See how you inspired me?"

I signaled Charlie to come join us and saw her whisper excitedly to Lauren, Brooke, Lily, and Jillian. Grabbing hands, they all bolted up to us and surrounded the governor like a hawk circling its prey.

"Over here, girls," Tyler called from the front row. "Look into the lens."

He didn't have to tell them twice, that's for sure. They were all over it, assuming their most extreme model poses and casting über-flirty glances at the camera. Jillian was the worst, raising her arms over her head and sticking her chest out like some Kim Kardashian wannabe.

Oh, wait. Jillian is a Kim Kardashian wannabe.

The only two sane-looking ones in the group were Governor Corday and Lily, who both smiled naturally at Tyler and didn't go completely nutso with the posing. Meanwhile, Tom Ballard was back at the microphone, thanking the governor for showing up and reminding people that if they cared about arts in the schools, they should vote for him in the next election.

Suddenly, the wail of sirens filled the air. One minute they weren't there, the next minute all you could hear was sirens, lots of them, approaching the club. Then a voice rang out in the crowd. It was Officer Beswick, speaking into a handheld megaphone from his position at the gate.

"Ladies and gentlemen, stay calm! We have the situation under control!"

If you want people to panic, all you have to do is tell them to stay calm. Everyone gasped and looked around desperately to see what was the matter. Two officers bolted out of the house and up to the stage, surrounding the governor like she was in immediate danger.

What was going on? I looked around frantically, first out at the black ocean, then back at the shore.

That was when I saw them. Flames. Huge, bright orange flames billowing out of Mrs. Ivanov's house.

"Fire!" someone yelled.

The crowd moved like a mob, surging toward the gate in a giant human wave.

"That old wooden house will burn like a matchstick!" I heard Dr. Mandel say.

"Remain calm," Officer Beswick repeated. "Clear the area. Move slowly away from the buildings."

"It's going to spread to the club," a panicky woman shouted.

The wind whipped around us, blowing red-hot embers into the night air.

"Santa Ana winds," Noah Mandel told his father. "Compressed air creates rising temperatures. Fire conditions."

"Sammie! Charlie!" It was my dad, running from the house to find us, followed by Ryan. "Come with me. We have to evacuate. It's not safe in the house."

"Mr. Diamond, have you seen Oscar and Eddie?" Alicia asked him, her voice full of worry.

"The police are moving everyone out to the parking lot," he answered. "That's probably where they are."

"Where's GoGo?" I hollered. The last I had seen her was right after the performance, when she had returned to the kitchen to bring out another platter of brownies.

My dad's eyes scanned the horizon, looking for

GoGo's distinctive gray hair, which she always puts in a knot on top of her head. Nothing. I stayed behind to look for her.

"GoGo!" I shouted at the top of my lungs. I squinted through the smoky air, trying to see into our kitchen window. She wasn't there.

"Where could she be?" Charlie cried, grabbing me by the arm.

Suddenly, it dawned on me. I knew where she was! Not that I had seen her, but I know my grandmother, and I figured out exactly what she would do in this situation. I broke loose from my dad and bolted across the deck toward Mrs. Ivanov's house. As I neared the flames, I could feel their heat on my face.

"Stay away, young lady," Officer Beswick called into his megaphone. "The firefighters will be here any second. Let them handle this."

The flames were concentrated in the front of the house, leaping out from the living room that faced the sandy beach. It was the room where Mrs. Ivanov had been sitting earlier that day when I brought her the meal from GoGo. She had been so happy and peaceful, resting in her white wicker rocking chair and looking through an old photo album. And now, that peaceful room was being consumed by flames!

I approached the house cautiously after Officer Beswick left to meet the firefighters, but was forced back when one of her blue-and-white-striped deck umbrellas caught on fire, exploding like a Roman candle on the Fourth of July.

"Mrs. Ivanov," I shouted above the roar of the fire. "Are you in there?"

"We're over here, Sammie."

It was GoGo's voice, coming from the side of the house. She was at the side door, very slowly making her way out. Holding on to her arm for dear life was Mrs. Ivanov, looking frail and frightened in her pink bathrobe.

"GoGo, you have to get out of there!" I screamed.

"The poor dear can't go any faster!" she yelled back.

Suddenly, I felt a strong, familiar arm push me aside.

"Clear the way, Sam-I-Am," Ryan said, swooping in from behind me. "I've got speed and height on my side."

He raced past me and in two seconds flat arrived at the side door. In one swift movement, he scooped Mrs. Ivanov up into his giant arms.

"I have you," he said to her, with no trace of his usual goofiness. "Hang on tight."

"But my photographs are inside," she cried. "My whole life."

"I'm so sorry, Mrs. Ivanov. We can't go back in there. It's too dangerous. GoGo, are you okay?"

"Take care of Mrs. Ivanov," she told him. "I'll follow right behind you!"

Ryan ran across the deck holding poor Mrs. Ivanov in his arms, while I raced over and grabbed GoGo by the hand. My dad was right on my heels and arrived just in time to scoop her into his arms. All of us ran away from the burning building, and were lucky enough to arrive in the safety of the parking lot unharmed. Charlie burst into tears when she saw that we were all okay.

"Is anyone else in that house?" the governor asked.

"I don't think so," I answered. "Mrs. Ivanov lives all alone."

Alicia came charging up to me, her voice desperate.

"I found Eddie. He was on the beach with the other boys. But I didn't see Oscar."

Two fire trucks arrived on the scene and pulled into the parking lot alongside us. In a matter of seconds, a swarm of firefighters descended from the trucks. There was a fire chief who hollered commands, and they got right to work, connecting their giant hoses to the pumper truck. Working in teams, they moved closer and closer to Mrs. Ivanov's house, pointing the streams of water directly at the flames. A few of them who weren't holding hoses crept up to the wooden house. Staying low to the ground, they got close enough to knock down the front door with axes. Flames shot out. The firefighters holding the hoses took aim and immediately bombarded them. We heard a loud sizzling sound and white smoke billowed from the doorway.

Over in the parking lot, the four police officers had formed a human chain to keep us away from the fire. They were encouraging people to get in their cars and leave. Most left, but some stayed. Dr. Mandel said he wanted to stay in case anyone needed emergency medical treatment.

Meanwhile, Alicia was maneuvering through the crowd, calling Oscar's name.

"You looking for the dude in the Human Torch sweatshirt?" Noah asked when she bumped into him.

"Yes, have you seen him?"

"Yeah, he was in that Ferrari. The one parked in front of the club."

Alicia came and got me and we ran to Tyler's car. Even in the darkness, I could see Oscar huddled inside, looking small and frightened. I pulled on the door handle, but it was locked, so I pounded on the window.

"Oscar, open up!"

He shook his head.

"Oscar, right now," Alicia yelled. "You can't stay in there."

He shook his head again.

"Oscar, there's a huge fire. What if it spreads? It's dangerous in there."

Oscar looked from Alicia to me. Slowly, he unlocked the car door and we pulled it open. I could see that there were tears rolling down his face.

"What are you doing in there?" Alicia demanded.

"I was just looking inside Tyler's Batmobile," he said. "He told me I could."

"Oscar, why are you crying?" Alicia asked him. "Tell us."

"The policeman, the mean one with the flashlight, he saw me inside here," he said, trying to stifle his sobs.

"That must be Officer Porter," I said.

"I don't know his name, but he yelled at me. He thought I was stealing the car. He pounded on the window, so I locked myself in."

"You should have just gotten out and explained everything to him," Alicia said.

"I was going to. Then suddenly, all the trucks and sirens came. The policeman, he ran away with them. But he said he'd be back. I was afraid of him. I was afraid of the fire. I didn't know what to do. So I stayed locked inside."

"You don't have to be afraid anymore, Oscar," I said to him. "You didn't do anything wrong."

"But that policeman, he thinks I did."

"He just didn't understand that you had Tyler's permission to look in his car," I said. "Come out. Come be with us. It's okay. Trust me, it's okay."

He got out of the car slowly, and I took him by the hand. I could feel that he was trembling all over. Alicia and I led him over to the deck. We sat him down at one of the redwood picnic tables. Alicia stayed with him while I went to find the governor, who was speaking with the fire chief while a few remaining guests were observing the firefighters. There were no more orange flames shooting from Mrs. Ivanov's house. Instead, clouds of white smoke wafted out of the water-soaked structure.

"It looks like we have it under control, ma'am," the fire chief said to Governor Corday.

"No danger of it spreading?" she asked.

"Not anymore. We were lucky, though. Lucky it didn't spread. Lucky the structure didn't collapse."

"So I can go home now?" Mrs. Ivanov asked. Ryan had put her gently in one of our beach chairs where she sat stunned, watching the fire.

Governor Corday pulled up a chair and sat down next to her. She spoke very softly to her.

"Mrs. Ivanov, you're not going to be able to go home for quite a while," she said. "The fire has seriously damaged a good part of your house."

"But my photographs, they are all right, yes?" Mrs. Ivanov was practically pleading. "I can't lose my photographs."

"I'm sure the firefighters will save everything they can," the governor reassured her.

"I love the one from *Swan Lake*," Mrs. Ivanov said with a faraway smile. "I danced with Rudolf Nureyev, you know. It was 1964 in Paris. He was such a handsome boy. And a beautiful prince."

The governor glanced at the fire chief.

"Is there any chance?" she whispered.

He shook his head. "I'm sorry. Everything in there is either burned or water-damaged."

"Oh no," Mrs. Ivanov said. "Oh no, oh no, oh no!"

And then she put her head in her small, delicate hands and wept.

"We'll find out what happened here," Governor Corday said, putting her arm around Mrs. Ivanov's thin shoulders. "I promise you that."

"Governor Corday," her chief aide said. He was holding two cell phones, one to each ear. "We have to go. You have two more appearances tonight."

"Cancel them, Chris," she said. Then turning to the fire chief, she asked, "Do you have any idea what started this fire? Was it the Santa Ana winds?"

"The winds didn't help," the chief answered. "But they didn't cause the fire. People did."

"People? What people?"

"Most likely kids. My men tell me they found a fresh bonfire on the beach in front of Mrs. Ivanov's house. In this wind, one spark from a bonfire can fly off, land on an old wood structure like this, and poof... it goes up in flames. Just like what happened here."

"But bonfires are illegal on this beach," the governor reminded him.

"Sure. Go tell that to the kids."

A bonfire! Immediately, I suspected Jared and Sean and the General. I had seen the two of them out on the beach earlier. And when we were doing our performance, they were nowhere to be seen. Probably making the bonfire they always talked about. I didn't say anything, though. First of all, I didn't have any evidence, just a suspicion. And second of all, I knew the truth would reveal itself.

"Do you have any suspects?" Governor Corday asked the chief.

"Yes, ma'am, we certainly do."

There, like I just said. The truth would reveal itself. Those boys would pay the price for breaking the rules.

"Officer Porter reported a young Latino kid who was acting suspiciously," the fire chief said. "He was hiding in a locked car and wouldn't come out. Apparently, he was wearing a sweatshirt with some kind of fire symbol on it."

Oscar? Was he talking about Oscar?

"Some kids are like that," he went on. "Obsessed with fire. Can't get enough of it. We're going to talk to him now."

I glanced over at the redwood table and saw Oscar sitting with Alicia. He looked so scared. Officers Beswick and Porter were approaching him, with Porter shining his flashlight right into Oscar's face.

Oh no, I thought. *Oh no, oh no, oh no!*

The Accusation

Chapter 12

"He didn't do it," I said to Governor Corday, planting my feet firmly in front of her. "I know he didn't."

From where I was standing, I could see Officer Porter questioning Oscar. I couldn't hear what he was saying, but I saw that Oscar wasn't answering. He just kept his head down and stared at the wooden planks on the deck. Alicia was sitting next to him with her arm around his shoulders. She was crying.

"Sammie, you can't say that for certain," Governor Corday said. "The fire chief said your friend was acting suspiciously."

"But, Governor, I am a Truth Teller. Even you said how brave I was to tell the truth, no matter how painful. I wouldn't lie about this."

"Listen to me, Sammie. Sometimes when we care about people, we want to believe the best about them. I understand that you want to believe your friend is innocent. But you have to let the officers do their work."

"Well, I'm going to help Oscar. He doesn't even know how to answer their questions."

"I'll come with you," she offered. "I want to get to the bottom of this, too. Let's just make sure that Mrs. Ivanov is settled first."

An ambulance had come to take Mrs. Ivanov to the hospital to be checked. She was protesting, saying that she was fine and wanted to stay in her house. It was only when GoGo agreed to ride in the ambulance with her that Mrs. Ivanov agreed to go. Governor Corday was so incredibly kind to Mrs. Ivanov. She even waited by the ambulance until she was settled on the gurney and safely inside.

"Please let me know how she is," the governor said to GoGo. "This must be heartbreaking for her."

Her aide handed GoGo a card with phone numbers on it. "You can reach us on the private line," he said.

"Sammie, you take care of Oscar," GoGo called out to me. "Get your father to help."

The ambulance driver closed the double doors, and the last thing I saw as it pulled away was GoGo reaching out to take Mrs. Ivanov's hand.

Governor Corday kept her promise. She told her

aide to hold all her calls, that she had urgent business she had to attend to. Together we went to the table where Oscar and Alicia were sitting. By then, the fire chief had joined Officer Beswick and Officer Porter. Councilman Ballard was there, too, with Spencer at his side. Dr. Mandel was sitting quietly, stroking his gray beard, his bushy eyebrows furrowed. Amidst all those important people, poor little Oscar looked frightened and alone.

For the first time since the fire broke out, I took a real look around. Mrs. Ivanov's house was damaged, but not as badly as I had thought. The front room and the deck were entirely scorched, but the back of the house seemed like it had been saved. Nearby, the firefighters were cleaning up the mess from the fire, picking up debris and carrying their hoses and equipment to the truck. Sitting at a table close to the beach, just a little distance from us, were Lauren and Charlie and the other girls. All their smiles had disappeared. They looked worried and jittery. I noticed that Jared, Sean, and the General had joined them. The only kids missing were Lily and Eddie. They were nowhere to be seen.

I had a desperate urge to march right over to Jared, Sean, and the General and accuse them of setting the bonfire. I wanted to make them defend themselves, to stand up for what I believed they had done. But they weren't the ones being encircled by a group of adults asking tough questions. Oscar was. And he needed my help. I had to pay attention to the questioning that was going on, so I turned away from them and focused my full attention on Governor Corday.

"What have you learned, gentlemen?" she asked as she took a seat at the redwood table.

"Not much," Officer Porter said. "The suspect isn't talking."

"He's not a suspect," I blurted out, trying to sound reasonable but knowing that I was barking like an angry little dog. "His name is Oscar Bermudez and he's here to get his leg operated on. Isn't that right, Dr. Mandel?"

"That's correct," he answered quietly. There was pain in his voice. "I hope we can still do that."

"We all feel for this young man and his physical difficulties," Mr. Ballard said. "But the issue here is whether or not he started the bonfire. The police have asked him, but he has refused to answer."

"That's because he's afraid of you," I said. "Of all of you."

"If he's innocent, he has nothing to be afraid of," Officer Beswick pointed out. Easy for him to say. He wasn't a thirteen-year-old kid from a country two thousand miles away with a bunch of powerful grown-ups breathing down his neck.

"Sammie, can I use your phone?" Alicia said. "I have to call my father. He should be here."

"That will take too long, Alicia. Go find my dad. He'll help."

She got up to look for my dad. Through the clubhouse window, I could see that he was on the phone. Ryan was next to him, writing something down on a yellow pad. I assumed they were trying to get the number of Oscar and Eddie's parents in El Salvador. Ryan's under the mistaken impression that he is actually good at speaking Spanish. My dad looked totally frustrated. I tried to get my dad's attention, but he didn't look up, just kept pacing back and forth with the phone to his ear. We needed him here, to defend Oscar, to tell Officer Porter to give Oscar a chance to speak.

"Oscar," Governor Corday said. "I know this is very intimidating. But we need to hear what you have to say. Will you talk to me? I'm not here to hurt you. I want to help."

Her voice was soft and soothing. For the first time, Oscar looked up from the ground. He glanced over at me.

"It's okay," I whispered to him. "She's a good person."

He nodded.

"Good," the governor said. "That's a start. Now Oscar, tell me honestly. Did you make that bonfire on the beach?"

"No."

"Then why are you wearing that sweatshirt that says 'The Human Torch'?" Officer Porter butted in. "Just for grins and giggles?"

"He's my favorite superhero," Oscar muttered. His voice was shaking.

"Oh, really? The Human Torch? What's he do?" Officer Porter's voice was harsh and accusing. "Set fire to old ladies' houses?"

"Officer Porter," the governor said. "Try to control yourself. You're frightening this young man."

Oscar looked back down at the ground. I could see him pulling back into his protective shell of silence.

I hate bullies. Every kind of bully. Grown-up bullies and kid bullies. Bullies in long basketball shorts or bullies in uniforms. As far as I'm concerned, they're just people who like to pick on others who can't defend themselves. I opened my mouth to confront Big Bully Porter, but Spencer beat me to it, and in a much more polite tone of voice than I was about to use.

"Officer Porter," he said in a calm and surprisingly mature voice. "The Human Torch is one of the Fantastic Four, like the Thing and Invisible Girl. They make the world better through scientific discovery. The Torch can control fire by sheer force of will. Right, Oscar?"

Oscar nodded and even gave the slightest grin of recognition. I could have kissed that Spencer Ballard.

"Poppycock comic book crud," Porter said.

"Maybe to you," Spencer said. "But kids like it, and that doesn't make us criminals."

"Thank you," the governor said to him. "Well said." Then turning to Oscar, she went on with her questioning. "Tell me, Oscar, where were you when the fire broke out?"

"In the Batmobile."

"Oh swell, now we have to listen to more comic book nonsense," Porter scoffed. "Why don't you let me ask a few questions, ma'am? I'll get to the bottom of this."

"Please let Oscar speak." The governor frowned at Office Porter. He tried to hide his annoyance, but I could see him tapping his foot impatiently. She went on. "Tell me, Oscar, what is the Batmobile?"

"It's a Ferrari 458 Spider convertible—Tyler's car."

"Tyler Frank is the photographer," I explained. "He said it was okay for Oscar to take a look inside his car. If you don't believe me, ask him."

I looked around to see if Tyler was there to put in a good word, but he was already gone.

"Where'd he go?" I asked.

"He left a few minutes ago," the governor's aide answered. "Said something about having to get the photos in before the deadline."

Great. He's no help.

"Oscar, did anyone see you in the car when the fire started?" Officer Beswick asked. He didn't seem like he was trying to blame Oscar; it was more like he wanted to help.

"No, sir. I was by myself."

"Where was Eddie?" Alicia asked. "Didn't he go with you?"

"He went for a walk on the beach. With Lily."

"So we have no eyewitnesses to verify that he was in the car at the time the bonfire was started," Officer Porter stated flatly. "All we have is his word, for what that's worth."

I could see all of the adults at the table exchanging glances. I didn't like where this was going. I looked over at Charlie, who was sitting at the table with her friends. They were all listening intently, except for a couple of the SF2 boys who had left their table. She was sitting with Lauren on one side and Jillian on the other. I wanted her to come sit next to me, to tell these people that Oscar was a good guy, that he would never harm anyone or anything. But when my eyes met Charlie's, she looked away. I thought I saw her scoot over closer to Lauren.

Someone had to defend Oscar, and it looked like it was up to me.

"You guys are not being fair," I said. "Just because no one saw Oscar in the car doesn't mean he started the bonfire."

"That's true, Sammie," Governor Corday answered. "However, it does mean that we can't account for his whereabouts when the fire started."

"Which means we can't eliminate him as a suspect," Officer Porter chimed in.

"But you don't have any proof," I protested.

"The girl has a point," Officer Beswick said. "We don't have any evidence."

From the corner of my eye, I saw Jared approaching us. He was carrying a backpack, a bright red one that I immediately recognized as Oscar's.

"Excuse me, sir," Jared said to Officer Porter. "My name is Jared McCain, and I'm a member here. I found this backpack out on the beach that I think belongs to the suspect. Maybe there's something in there that would help you figure this out."

"Thanks for keeping your eyes open, son," Officer Porter said. He took the backpack and unzipped it, taking out its contents and laying each object on the table one by one. A half-empty bottle of water, a beat-up copy of *Car and Driver* magazine, a *Fantastic Four* comic book, a pack of colored pencils, and a folded-up drawing of the Human Torch rescuing that same blond girl from a burning skyscraper. It wasn't finished, but this time the girl looked more like me. At the very bottom of the backpack, there was a clean pair of white socks, and . . . could it be? . . . a pack of matches from Frankie's Clam Shack.

"Well, what do we have here?" Officer Porter said, holding up the matches for everyone to see. "Interesting, isn't it?"

Oscar couldn't believe his eyes.

"Those aren't mine!" he said.

"Oh, really?" Officer Porter snapped. "What did they do, walk into your backpack all by themselves?"

We all waited for Oscar to offer some explanation, but he didn't say a word.

"It's not against the law to carry matches," I said. "Just because he has them, doesn't mean he used them to start a fire. He's here from El Salvador. I'm sure he just took them as a souvenir. Didn't you, Oscar?"

"I already told you, they aren't mine," Oscar said. "Why doesn't anyone believe me?"

"All right, folks, I have a suggestion," the fire chief said, rising to his feet. "Everyone sit tight here for a minute. I'm going to check something out. I'll be right back."

We sat there waiting in silence, watching him walk across the deck and out onto the sand. In the darkness, we couldn't see what he was doing, but we followed his flashlight until it stopped at a place on the beach right in front of Mrs. Ivanov's house. I was so focused on watching him, I nearly jumped out of my skin when my dad slid onto the bench next to me.

"Been on the phone for twenty minutes," he said. "Finally, it's all arranged."

"What is, Dad?"

"Your match tomorrow," he said. "The Sand and Surf Club didn't know if they'd have to cancel the tournament because of the fire, but everything's a go. You girls play your first match at eleven."

He had to be kidding! With all that was going on, with Oscar in such terrible trouble, he expected me to play in some tennis tournament?

Is it possible that someone can have mashed potatoes for brains? Talk about a one-track mind!

I was just about to let him know that tennis was not on my next day's agenda, when the fire chief came tromping back across the sand to our table. His face looked stern. Troubled. He gave Oscar an unsympathetic look.

"I found these in the sand next to the bonfire pit," he said. And reaching into the pocket of his yellow jacket, he pulled out a charred pack of matches and tossed them on the table. Everyone leaned in to look at them. The cardboard cover was black around the edges and covered with ashes, but when you brushed away the soot, you could clearly read the words— Frankie's Clam Shack.

I gasped. Alicia gasped. Oscar gasped.

Governor Corday reached out and took my hand. "I'm so sorry, Sammie," she said. "It's terrible to be disappointed by a friend." Then she turned to the others. "Gentlemen, you can take it from here."

I watched her leave and climb into the black limousine that had been waiting for her all this time. When she was gone, I turned to check on Oscar. I looked into his beautiful dark eyes. They were filled with sorrow and shame.

This is as bad as it gets.

Little did I know, the worst was yet to come.

The Worst News Ever

Chapter 13

"We're going to send you home with your uncle tonight," Officer Beswick said to Oscar. "There's not much we can do in the dark. Tomorrow we'll continue the investigation."

Alicia had finally gotten in touch with Candido, who came barreling over in his truck in record time. When Oscar saw him, he fell into his arms and sobbed. They spoke in Spanish, and although I couldn't understand the words, I could see that Candido was trying to calm him down and reassure him. By that time, Eddie and Lily had returned from their walk. They had strolled all the way down to the Santa Monica Pier and even gone for a ride on the Ferris wheel. When Ryan brought Eddie up to speed on what had happened, he got really upset that he hadn't seen the fire or been there to protect and defend Oscar. Lily put her hand on his arm.

"I'm sure this is all a misunderstanding," she said to Eddie.

"Don't be so sure of that," Officer Porter said. "These kids aren't like you and your friends. Chances are, they don't even know right from wrong."

"You have no reason to say that," Lily said. "It's unfair to judge people before you know anything about them."

"No offense, honey," Officer Porter said, "but you don't know what you're talking about."

Lily bit her lip to keep from saying more. Instead, she turned to Eddie and whispered, "I'm sorry you have to hear this. The rest of us don't feel that way. At least, I don't."

Officer Beswick wrote down an address and handed the piece of paper to Candido.

"I want you at the police station at ten o'clock tomorrow," he said to Candido and Oscar. "By that time, our investigators will have gathered up any other evidence and we can see where we are with this."

"Do you think we can trust you to be there?" Officer Porter asked Candido.

I had never seen Candido get angry before. He always has the sweetest smile on his face, and is so nice to everyone at the club, especially the kids. When their beach balls go into the water or the sand is too hot on their little feet, he stops to help them, no matter what else he's doing. But there was no doubt that Officer Porter had made him really angry, and I didn't blame him one bit.

"We will be there," Candido said, his tone of voice sharp and abrupt. "You believe my nephew is guilty, but I believe he is innocent."

"You're entitled to your opinion, mister," Officer Porter said with a shrug. "But you can't argue with evidence."

"We will be there," Candido said. "You have my word."

Rising to his full height, he put on his straw cowboy hat and turned to leave. Eddie and Alicia followed him. Oscar got up to go, too. I ran after him, and when I reached him, I put my body in front of his so he couldn't leave without talking to me.

"Oscar, look at me. I know you didn't cause that fire."

"But I have caused all this trouble for you, Sammie. I should never have come to America."

"Don't say that. You came here to get your leg fixed. We'll show them that you're innocent."

"How?"

That was a good question.

"I don't know, Oscar. I just know that I believe in you."

He looked so sad, so hurt. Before I could even think about what I was doing, I leaned over and kissed him on the cheek. He put his hand up to his face and touched the spot gently. I took his hand in mine, but he pulled it away from me.

"No, Sammie. I am too ashamed."

Then he stepped around me and followed the others to the truck. As I watched him go, it seemed that he was limping more than usual. I understood. He was weighed down with a lot of worry.

Alicia and Eddie were already in the backseat of the truck and Candido was behind the wheel with the engine running, waiting for Oscar to climb into the front so they could go home.

"Candido! Wait up a second!" a voice called. "We have to talk."

I turned around to see Dr. Mandel hurrying out of the club and over to the truck. I followed him, and when he reached the passenger side door, Oscar rolled down the window. Dr. Mandel was a little out of breath and seemed . . . I don't know . . . frazzled.

"I hate to be the one to bring you this news, I really do," he said.

Everything inside of me wanted to cover my ears and shout, so that I wouldn't have to hear what he was about to say. When Charlie and I were little and it was bedtime, we'd cover our ears and yell "peas and carrots" over and over again so we wouldn't have to hear my mom tell us it was bedtime. If only I could have shouted "peas and carrots" right into Dr. Mandel's worried face.

"I'm afraid we have to postpone the surgery," he said.

"Postpone?" Oscar asked. "What does that mean?"

"It means we can't do it this Tuesday, Oscar."

"What day will you do it?"

Dr. Mandel sighed. "We have to wait and see what happens, Oscar. I've contacted the hospital board, and given the circumstances, they don't feel they're able to grant the money."

"But they were able to grant it yesterday," I said. "What happened?"

"It's a fifty thousand-dollar commitment from the hospital," Dr. Mandel said to me. He was clearly uncomfortable, struggling for the right words. "That's a lot of money. It has to go to . . . to a . . . deserving . . . individual. They just don't feel that Oscar would be a good candidate at this moment."

"Because of the fire?" Candido asked. "He didn't do anything wrong."

"Well, Candido, we don't know that for sure." Dr. Mandel could hardly look at Candido. "And until we do, we just have to put the surgery on hold."

"But, Dr. Mandel," Alicia pleaded from the backseat, "Oscar is counting on it. It means everything to him to get his foot fixed. He's waited for this his whole life."

Dr. Mandel nodded. He seemed genuinely choked up.

"My hands are tied. All I can do is hope everything works out for the best," he said softly. "I'm so sorry, Oscar."

He shook his head and walked away. I couldn't even bring myself to look into Oscar's eyes. I knew the pain and disappointment I'd see there would be too much to bear. I searched desperately for some words that would be reassuring, comforting, anything.

But the sad truth was, there was nothing more to say.

A Terrible Secret

....

Chapter 14

"I hope you're happy," I snapped, marching up to the table on the deck where the SF2 kids were sitting. "Oscar's surgery has been canceled."

They were all there but Spencer, who was helping his dad record the donation checks and put them into envelopes. Ryan had joined them a few minutes before when he noticed that they were finishing off the leftover brownies. Lauren had moved from her seat next to Charlie and was trying to snuggle up on the bench next to Ryan. He was more interested in snuggling up to the platter of brownies.

"It's been canceled, or postponed?" Ryan asked, talking, as usual, with his mouth full.

"Dr. Mandel said postponed, but I think it's just a nice way of saying canceled."

"What a drag," Brooke said. "Now Oscar's going to be stuck wearing those creepy shoes forever."

"Yeah, that sucks," the General agreed.

The thing about Brooke Addison and her fake military boyfriend is that way down deep, they're shallow. I mean, in the end, it's all about the shoes.

"Poor Oscar," Charlie said quietly. "What happened, Sammie?"

"The hospital won't pay for the operation. They think he's not a deserving candidate. And why? Because he's getting blamed for something he didn't do."

I glared at Jared, trying to look like every tough-talking lawyer I had ever seen on TV. The difference is, when mean lawyers on TV do that, the guilty person breaks down and confesses. In my case, Jared just sneered at me.

"Whoa there, you," Sean Patterson said to me, draping a friendly arm over his pal Jared's shoulder. "The police found the matches in his backpack. The same matches that lit the fire. How do you explain that, Little Miss Hothead?"

"Speaking of whoa there," Ryan said, "you might want to ease up on the name calling, Patterson. I am the only one entitled to call Sammie names. It's off limits for the rest of you tots."

I appreciated the support, but I was just getting started.

"I think everyone here knows that Oscar didn't

start that bonfire," I said. "You guys have been talking about making a bonfire for the last month. I've heard you myself. It's not exactly a coincidence that a bonfire was started when you were all here."

"We couldn't have done it," Lauren said. "We were watching you. And getting our picture taken with the governor."

"And tomorrow, we'll have the pictures to prove it," Jillian said. "Speaking of which, I hope this fire thing doesn't ruin our chances of getting on magazine covers."

"Actually, Jilly, I think it helps," Lauren whispered. "I can see the headlines now. Attractive teen girls help save old woman's house."

"What are you talking about?" I snapped. "You didn't do anything to save Mrs. Ivanov's house."

"That's not true," Brooke said. "I personally walked over there and carried one of her potted geraniums to safety. And I might add, that little act of heroism ruined my new suede flats. They got all soaked from that gross fire-hose water."

There's only one word for her. Hopeless.

"What about you guys?" I asked, turning to Sean, Jared, and the General. "You could have done it. Where were you when the bonfire was started?"

"I was with Brooke," the General said.

"And looking cute as always," she said.

"And you two?" I said, turning to Jared and Sean. I didn't have proof that they were guilty, but I felt in my bones they were. Besides, I had seen them out on the beach right near that spot earlier.

"What are you, a cop?" Sean said. "Where we were is none of your business."

"Why don't you just do the right thing and confess?" I said, getting right up in their faces.

"There's nothing to confess to," Jared snarled. "You saw the matches in Oscar's backpack. He did it. Just because you have a crush on him and you don't think he can do anything wrong, you go around accusing us."

"Eeuuwww," Jillian said. "You have a crush on *him*?" Then she burst out laughing. "Honestly, Sammie, you are such a loser."

Lily had been very quiet during this conversation, just sitting there and taking it all in. But when Jillian laughed at the thought that anyone could have a crush on Oscar, she rose to her feet.

"Jillian, did anyone ever tell you that you have a very mean streak in you?" she said, picking up her purse and throwing it over her shoulder.

"Huh?" Jillian answered. "Lil, what's got into you?"

"All of us have been so quick to judge people based on nothing but how they look," Lily fumed. "That police officer did it, and we're guilty, too. I include myself in that. I mean, I went after Eddie because he's handsome. That was the first and most important thing I noticed. Appearances don't tell you the whole story about a person, though. It wasn't until I spent some real time with him tonight that I learned he's as good on the inside as he is on the outside. But none of us ever gave Oscar a chance."

"Don't go all mental on us, Lily," Jared said. "We're the same people we've always been."

"Maybe that's the problem," she said. "Sammie was the only one who saw that Oscar is really cool in his own way. The rest of us behaved like snobs. Personally, I'm done with that."

I was totally surprised to hear her say that. The SF2s are known for sticking together, for being loyal to each other no matter what. This was the first time I had seen one of them break with the group and take a stand.

"Okay, listen up, guys," Jared said. "It's really late and we've been through a lot. Let's break up this little party before we all join Lily and freak out and say things we'll regret later."

"Fine, I'm happy to leave," Lily said. "But I don't regret saying what I did. And I won't later, either."

That for sure ended the conversation. The girls found Chip Wadsworth, who was inside helping my dad fill out police reports. The boys each found their own parents, who were straightening up the kitchen since GoGo wasn't there to do it. Mr. Ballard and Spencer finished counting the money and announced that in spite of everything, the evening had been a success. We had raised over sixteen thousand dollars to donate to the arts programs in our schools. Given what had happened to Oscar, raising that money felt weird to me. How could something so wonderful and so awful happen at the very same time?

All the SF2s and their parents gathered their things and headed for the parking lot. Ryan and I watched as the parade of shiny black cars pulled out onto Pacific Coast Highway and headed to Santa Monica. There must be an unwritten rule that to be a member of the Sporty Forty, you have to drive a shiny black car. I have yet to see even one measly cream-colored car in the parking lot. And red is totally out of the question.

The Wadsworths were the last to leave. Charlie hung out with Lauren, Jillian, and Brooke, leaning on the side of their car and whispering until the very last minute when Chip Wadsworth climbed into the front seat and turned on the headlights. He's president of the Sporty Forty, and I guess he felt like it was his duty to double check that everything was safe and locked up. He takes his presidential responsibilities very seriously. I hope you never have to see how furious he gets when someone has the nerve to leave a towel draped over the back of one of the beach chairs.

"I'm going to pick up GoGo at the hospital," our dad said when the Wadsworth's car was finally out of sight. "She called to say that Mrs. Ivanov is okay, but they're going to keep her overnight for observation. Hopefully, she can leave tomorrow."

"Where will she go?" I asked.

"Apparently she has a sister in San Diego. She's going to live with her until her house is repaired."

"Are they going to be able to fix it?" Charlie wondered.

"Walter McCain says yes."

"Jared's father?" Charlie asked. That seemed to catch her interest.

"He owns a construction company," my dad replied, nodding. "He told me that front room is pretty badly damaged, and the deck is shot. He thinks the damages might run into the tens of thousands of dollars. But it's a historic house, so it's worth repairing."

"I feel so bad," Charlie said, tearing up. "Mrs. Ivanov lost all her pictures. That stuff can't ever be replaced."

Suddenly, she burst into tears, which I thought was very strange. Charlie and I, being identical twins, often share many of the same feelings. We cry at the same movies, get choked up when we see moms and babies together, and even get all emotional if we see someone kill a spider. But thinking about Mrs. Ivanov's loss didn't make me want to cry at all. It made me mad, fuming mad.

"You're overtired, Charlie," my dad said. "That's why you're so emotional. You girls get right to bed. You have to be rested for your tournament tomorrow. We'll leave at ten, but I want you warming up at nine."

"We can't go, Dad," I announced matter-of-factly.

"Of course you can. Why can't you go?"

"Because I have to be at the police station tomorrow at ten. I have to be there to support Oscar."

He sighed deeply.

"Sammie, Oscar has made his own bed. He has to lie in it."

"What's that supposed to mean?"

"It means that he has to accept the consequences for whatever he's done. And while you can feel bad for him, those consequences are his and cannot affect your life in a negative way."

"Wait, wait, Dad. Are you saying you believe he's guilty?"

"I'm saying they found matches in his backpack, Sammie. I think there are reasonable assumptions that follow from that."

I flopped down on the living room couch and watched him grab his car keys and leave. For the first time that night, I began to question myself. Was I the only one who believed Oscar was innocent? Why was I holding on to that? I mean, I hadn't actually seen Jared and Sean set the fire. And they truly did find those matches in Oscar's backpack. But Oscar had said they weren't his. He looked me right in the eye and said they weren't his. He was a Truth Teller. I felt that deep in my heart.

Charlie was still very teary as we got ready for bed. She stayed in the bathroom a long time, blowing her nose every thirty seconds. When she came out, her eyes and nostrils were all red.

"Are you okay?" I asked her.

She shrugged, then climbed into her bed and rolled over with her back to me. I could see her rubbing little circles on her face with the satin edge of her blanket, something she's done to soothe herself to sleep since she was a baby.

"I feel bad for Oscar," she said as I turned out the light. "It's so sad."

"It's not sad, Charlie. It's tragic. Flat-out tragic."

She was silent. After a long while, she asked, "Do you really think they're not going to do the operation?"

"They won't if they think he set that fire. Even if Dr. Mandel would do it, the hospital people won't allow it."

"But it was an accident. I'm sure nobody meant for Mrs. Ivanov's house to catch on fire."

In the dark, I could hear that Charlie was crying again. I sat up and turned on the lights.

"Charlie, look at me."

"What?" she said, her back still to me.

"Is there something you know? About the . . . um . . . accident? Something that would help Oscar?"

"Don't make me do this, Sammie. Please."

"Charlie. If there is something you know that you're not saying, something that would help prove Oscar's innocence, then you have to say it. This is no small thing we're talking about. This is something that will affect him every day for his whole life. Do you want that on your conscience?"

Charlie turned to face me and started to cry again. "I just don't know what to do," she said, weeping.

"What is the problem here, Charles?"

Her lip was quivering as she spoke. "They told me I couldn't double-cross them."

"Double-cross who, Charlie? I don't understand."

"Lauren and the girls. They said that I couldn't tell anyone. Out by the car . . . they made me promise. They said that SF2s don't double-cross each other. That we stick together. And that if I told, I couldn't be one of them anymore."

She held her head in her hands and cried so hard her shoulders were shaking. "I don't want Oscar to be crippled his whole life. But I don't want to be a double-crosser, either."

I got out of bed and sat on the edge of hers. I tried to look her in the eyes, but she dodged my look.

"Charlie," I said softly. "This isn't about Oscar or me or the SF2s. It's about doing the right thing. You know what that is. We both do."

"But what if they won't be my friends anymore? What if Spencer hates me, too?"

"Spencer seems like a decent guy," I said. "I bet he'll stand by you. And as for the others, true friends help you do the right thing. If they can't do that, then they're not really your friends."

She sat up on her bed and gradually stopped crying. I didn't say another word, just silently hoped and prayed that this was the sister I knew, the sister I loved, had always loved ever since I could remember.

"It was Jared and Sean," she said in a voice so full of emotion that it cracked when she spoke. "They started the fire. Then Jared found Oscar's backpack and put the matches in there so he'd get blamed."

"He planted those matches?"

"Yes."

How could he? Her words filled me with rage, an anger so wild I thought it would blow up in my chest.

"What kind of person does a thing like that?" I exploded.

"I don't know, Sammie."

"Well I know one thing, Charlie. I know what kind of person does what you just did. A brave person. A strong person. A good person."

"So you don't think I'm a bad friend? That I double-crossed them?"

I reached out and hugged her hard.

"You didn't double-cross anyone," I whispered to her. "You saved a life. And that's not just a great thing to do. It's pretty darn double great."

The Police Station

....

Chapter 15

"You girls don't look like you're dressed for a tennis tournament," my dad said, glancing up from his toast and orange juice. Although Charlie and I never dress alike except for our tennis matches, for some reason we both appeared at breakfast the next morning wearing jeans and red tops. They say that red is the color of power. Maybe we were both feeling powerful. I know I was, anyway.

"We're not going," I said, giving GoGo a hello kiss.

"How's Mrs. Ivanov?" Charlie asked.

"Shaken," GoGo answered, "but fortunately, her sister will take good care of her."

"Excuse me, ladies," Dad said, "but we're off topic here. I believe the topic is today's tennis tournament at the Sand and Surf Club."

"That topic is closed, Dad," I said. "We're not going. Tell him, Charlie."

"Um . . . Sammie thinks I need to come with her."

"Charlie," I said. "We discussed this. We agreed."

"Right." She nodded. Then clearing her throat to try to sound more sure of herself, she said, "Sammie and I have someplace we have to go."

"Hmmm, this will be an interesting breakfast," GoGo commented, giving us both a wink as she poured us two glasses of orange juice.

"I thought we discussed this yesterday," my dad said. "And I believe I came to the conclusion that your future tennis career takes precedence over other matters."

"That was yesterday," I said. "Yesterday was a whole different day, wasn't it, Charlie?"

"I guess so," she said quietly.

"Suppose we stop talking in riddles and you girls tell me what's going on."

"There is new evidence in the case of Oscar Bermudez," I explained. "Evidence that only Charlie and I can provide. Which means we have to be at the police station at ten."

"Sammie says it's a matter of life and death," Charlie added.

"Sammie, must you always be so overdramatic?" my dad said, sighing and putting down his newspaper.

"Dad, listen. They've canceled Oscar's surgery because they think he started the fire. We have to prove he's innocent. So you see, it is life and death. At least, the next closest thing."

GoGo picked up the telephone and handed it to my dad.

"Excuse me, Rick. I think you have a match to cancel," she said.

"So you're on their side, too?" He wasn't happy with her.

"I am always on the side of life," she answered. "And deep down, Rick, I know you are, too."

"I suppose you want me to drive you there, too," he grumbled, taking the phone from GoGo and dialing the number.

"Yes, please," I said.

As we gathered our purses and got ready to go, Charlie seemed worried.

"I hope they don't all hate me for ratting them out," she said.

"You're not ratting them out, Charlie. You're helping Oscar."

"But what if I can't say the words? Can't actually spit them out? I've never done anything like this before."

"Look at Oscar when you're talking. Look at Eddie. Look at Alicia and Candido. Look at their whole family and see how you're helping them."

"Okay, okay," she said. "I get the picture. Let's get on with this before I change my mind or pass out."

The Santa Monica police station takes up the first floor of City Hall. I had been there once on a second-grade field trip when we got to look inside a real police car and see the 911 operators in action. It's not at all scary like the dingy, dangerous police stations you see on TV crime shows. In fact, it's very light and airy, with a mural of the ocean and palm trees painted all along the lobby wall. As we sat there waiting for Candido to arrive, I told Charlie to concentrate on the mural and imagine that she was floating in a warm ocean wave. She was a bundle of nerves and needed to relax.

Candido arrived at exactly ten o'clock. He was wearing a gray suit and tie. Oscar and Eddie were wearing their dress-up clothes, too—the same ones they wore to the Truth Tellers dress rehearsal. Their hair was slicked back. Alicia was wearing a pleated skirt and a navy jacket I had never seen before, and her hair was held neatly back with a matching blue headband. If it weren't for the sad and worried look on each of their faces, you would have thought the whole Bermudez family was going to church.

Officers Porter and Beswick came out to greet us.

Officer Beswick politely escorted us from the lobby into a glassed-in conference room with a long table and chairs. Officer Porter followed behind. Sitting at the head of the table was a uniformed officer with gray hair pulled into a bun on the top of her head.

"This is Sergeant Turrisi," Officer Beswick said. "She's overseeing the investigation of the fire."

Sergeant Turrisi stood up and shook each of our hands.

"This is an unfortunate thing we're dealing with," she said, "but we're here to get to the bottom of the matter. Is everyone present who needs to be?"

"Actually," I said, "I think we should have two more people present."

Sergeant Turrisi looked surprised.

"And who might they be?" she asked.

"Jared McCain and Sean Patterson," I said. "I brought their home phone numbers with me."

I walked over and handed her the piece of paper. As I passed Charlie, I could see that she was slumped down in her chair, holding her stomach like she had a terrible stomachache.

"And why do you think these two gentlemen need to be here?" Sergeant Turrisi asked.

I waited for Charlie to answer, but she didn't say a word. Her face looked positively gray.

"Um, would it be okay if we talk to you in private?" I asked Sergeant Turrisi.

Without a word, she got up from the table and

headed into a glassed-in office that was right off the conference room. We followed her and went inside while she closed the door and leaned on her desk, her arms folded.

"Now what is it you have to say?" she asked.

"My sister and I have evidence that the two boys whose names are on that paper started the fire," I said.

Sergeant Turrisi turned to Charlie.

"Is this true?" she asked her.

Charlie made a sound that wasn't a definite yes or no. It was kind of a cross between a groan and a grunt.

"Excuse me, Ms. Diamond?"

Charlie looked up at me and I could see panic in her eyes.

"You can't back down now," I said to her.

Taking a deep breath, she nodded and turned to Sergeant Turrisi. "Yes," she said. "We have evidence."

"I'll need something more specific than that, Ms. Diamond."

Charlie looked over at me again, her eyes almost begging for me to let her off the hook. But I couldn't. It wasn't right.

"You have to say what you know," I told her.

Charlie took a deep breath and blurted it all out in one gush. She told the sergeant everything Lauren had told her, including how the boys had planted the matches in Oscar's backpack.

"These are very serious accusations," the sergeant said when Charlie had finished.

"That's why we think they should be here," I said.

"People certainly have a right to face their accuser." She nodded. "And to tell their side of the story. Follow me."

Sergeant Turrisi left the office and headed back to the conference room, where everyone was still sitting at the long table, probably wondering what was going on. She handed the piece of paper to Officer Beswick.

"See if you can call these families and ask them to bring their boys to the station right away," she said to him. Then turning to the rest of us, she added, "I have some paperwork I can take care of in the meantime. We will resume as soon as they get here."

She got up and left the room without so much as a good-bye or see you later. She was a no-nonsense kind of person.

"What's going on?" Alicia asked.

"We told her we thought Sean and Jared should be here."

"Do you think they'll come?" Oscar asked.

"I know this," my dad said, "if they were my kids, I wouldn't give them any choice in the matter. You cooperate with the police."

"They're not going to be happy about this," Eddie commented.

That did it for Charlie.

"I have to go to the bathroom," she said.

"Okay," I answered. "But you better come back. You can't chicken out now."

"I know this is the right thing to do, Sammie. It's just so hard. My friends mean a lot to me."

"If they're really your friends, they'll support you doing the right thing."

She nodded and gave me a weak little smile before leaving the room.

I sat there staring at the big clock on the wall. Oscar was fidgeting nervously, and jumped every time the hand clicked to the next number. Charlie stayed in the bathroom a long time, and I have to confess, I was very relieved when she came back.

A half hour passed, and neither the McCains nor the Pattersons showed up. My dad was busy checking his e-mail on his phone. Candido took out a comb and slicked back his hair at least three times. Oscar sat there playing with the laces on his shoes. I wanted to say something to him, to tell him that everything was going to be okay. But that would have been a lie. I wasn't sure at all that everything was going to be okay. Another fifteen minutes passed, and finally, Sergeant Turrisi returned to the conference room where we were sitting.

"I'm told that the young men in question have arrived at the station," she said. "Officer Porter is escorting them in."

Charlie let out a little sound that sounded like a gasp. I reached out and took her hand, hoping to give her strength. I knew this was going to be hard for her.

The first to enter were Mr. McCain and Mr.

Patterson. The two dads were wearing their tennis clothes, all white of course, with collars on their shirts. They did not look happy. In fact, they looked deeply annoyed. Sergeant Turrisi didn't seem to care, though. She stood up and quickly greeted them.

Then she looked at Jared and Sean, who lagged behind their fathers, obviously not wanting to be there. Jared and Sean were in their usual saggy-baggy basketball shorts, wearing sneakers with no socks and their shoes untied. I'm sorry, but you'd think when the police call you and tell you to come to the station, you could kick it up a notch and not look like you just rolled in from the gym.

"What's this about?" Mr. McCain said as they all blustered in and took a seat.

"Last night's fire on the beach," Officer Beswick said.

"I assume you need our boys to testify about what they found in that kid's backpack," Mr. Patterson said. "Okay, but if we can make it quick, we'd sure appreciate it. We've got court times booked."

"Sergeant Turrisi," I said, "my sister and I would like to testify first, if that's all right with you."

"This isn't a trial, Ms. Diamond," she answered. "No one is testifying here. We are merely conducting an investigation. Gathering information."

"I understand," I said.

"And I'm the one in charge here," Sergeant Turrisi continued.

I nodded and took a deep breath.

Sergeant Turrisi thumbed through the papers that were sitting in a folder on the table. "Now, the report states that these matches were from the same establishment as those found at the scene of the bonfire." She gave Oscar a suspicious look. "That is not a very favorable finding for you, young man."

"My sister has something to say about that, ma'am," I said.

"Yes, I know," Sergeant Turrisi answered. Then turning to Charlie, she said, "You seem reluctant to speak up, Ms. Diamond. Have you had second thoughts about your accusations?"

I looked at Charlie and motioned for her to speak. This was her moment. This was the time.

She looked over at Jared and Sean. Sean didn't return her look, but Jared did. He stared her down confidently, with the cocky, superior smile that was his trademark.

Charlie opened her mouth to speak, then closed it again. There was panic in her eyes as she looked at me. She looked down and fidgeted with her hands in her lap. Then she opened her mouth . . . and closed it again.

Come on, Charlie. This is no time to do your impression of a goldfish blowing bubbles. Say something.

"Charlie," my dad said, leaning toward her. "This isn't like you."

Still she was silent.

Mr. McCain cleared his throat impatiently and pointed to his watch.

"Uh . . . two words," he said. "Court times."

Sergeant Turrisi gave him an extremely irritated look.

"I'm sorry if the pursuit of justice interferes with your tennis game, Mr. McCain," she said. "How thoughtless of us."

You rock, Sergeant Turrisi.

Her remark seemed to give Charlie the courage she needed to speak up.

"Those matches did not belong to Oscar," she said, the words rushing out of her mouth like a torrent of water from a dam. "Jared put them in his backpack to make it seem like Oscar started the fire. But it was Jared and Sean who did it. Those two boys sitting over there."

She held up her shaking hand and pointed a finger at them. Sean slunk down low in his chair, but not Jared. He looked defiantly at her.

"Says who?" he asked.

"Lauren Wadsworth," she answered. "And Brooke Addison. The General told Brooke that you planted the matches. And Brooke told Lauren and Lauren told me."

"That's preposterous," Mr. McCain said. "Sergeant, these girls are making this up. My son is not capable of that kind of behavior."

"Sit down, Mr. McCain," Sergeant Turrisi said. "Let your son speak for himself, please. Tell me, Jared. Is any of this true?"

"Not a word," Jared answered. "They're making this up to protect him." He pointed at Oscar. "They just feel sorry for him, so they accused me. Us. Because we don't have anything wrong with us."

"That's not true and you know it," I shouted. "And besides, there's plenty wrong with you."

"Young lady, that's enough," Sergeant Turrisi said. Then she directed her attention to Charlie. "You've made some powerful accusations here. Do you have any proof of your claim?"

"Yes," Charlie answered. "I already told you. The General told Brooke, who is his girlfriend. And then Brooke told Lauren. They have no reason to lie."

"That's called hearsay," the sergeant said, "which is information gathered by one person from another person. It's not evidence. It's just hearsay."

"I don't care what you call it," Charlie said. "It's true. I swear it." She was practically crying.

"It's nothing more than teenagers gossiping," Officer Porter butted in. "Not worth a thing. You have no proof, honey. Face it."

Jared smiled smugly. Even Sean was sitting straighter in his chair, the old confidence returning. Suddenly, we heard someone knocking on the glass wall of the room. All eyes turned to see who could be interrupting this meeting. It was Tyler Frank, pounding on the window to be let in.

"Does anyone know that man?" Sergeant Turrisi asked.

"He's Tyler Frank," my dad answered. "The photographer hired to shoot pictures at the event last night."

Tyler stuck his head in the door.

"Excuse me for making such a rude entrance," he said. "I went to the club to find you guys, and a lady named GoGo told me you were here. I want to show you some photographs." Then he glanced over at Oscar and gave him a big smile. "How's things in Gotham?" he said.

"Very bad," Oscar answered. It was the first time he had spoken all morning.

"Not to worry, my man. They're about to get better," Tyler told him.

"Mr. Frank, we are in the middle of an investigative hearing," Sergeant Turrisi said. "I'm afraid your photographs will have to wait until some other time."

"But they pertain to this investigation," Tyler said. "You see, Sergeant, after the party I was at my studio reviewing the shots like I always do, picking out which ones I was going to send to the papers and magazines. And I found these. Just take a look. I printed them big so you could see them clearly."

He reached into his camera bag, pulled out about fifteen eight-by-ten photographs, and spread them out on the table.

"These are shots of the Truth Tellers performance," he said, "just after the governor arrived. Most of the images are of her or the kids. But as I was flipping through them, I noticed that some of them included the beach in the background. No magazine cares about seeing too much beach, so I enlarged the shot in order to remove most of the background. And while I was photoshopping it, I noticed this."

He held up a couple of the photographs, and there in the background, you could see two hazy figures hunched over a spot on the beach in front of Mrs. Ivanov's house.

"I enlarged those, and then I got these images." Tyler held up two more photographs. "As you can see, there is clearly a hole in the sand in which these figures have placed a pile of driftwood. The preparations for a bonfire."

He held up the next two photographs.

"And here are those same two figures lighting the driftwood. One of them is holding the match, the other is fanning the flames."

Everyone leaned in close to examine the photographs. And there they were in living color— Jared and Sean. Jared held the match. Sean was fanning the flames.

Oscar broke out into a smile as big as all of California. I wanted to stand up and hoot, but I was sure if I did, Officer Porter would arrest me for creating a public disturbance. Sergeant Turrisi picked up the photos and studied them for a full minute.

"Now this," she said, turning to Charlie, "this is not hearsay. This is called evidence. Proof."

Tyler held up his hand and high-fived Oscar.

"Batman to the rescue," he said. Oscar laughed. Man, oh, man, was that ever good to hear.

Sean slumped over and put his head on his knees. Jared shot a sidelong glance at his father, who had turned bright red in the face and looked like he was going to blow his top any minute. Finally, finally, finally, that cocky grin disappeared from Jared's face.

Sorry, Mr. McCain, looks like you're going to have to cancel that court time.

"Young men, do you have anything to say for yourselves?" Sergeant Turrisi asked, looking sternly at Jared and Sean.

"It was an accident," Sean said weakly. "We were just having fun."

"Accidents happen," the sergeant said. "But blaming someone else for damages that you caused, that is not an accident. That's just plain wrong."

"What's going to happen to us?" Jared asked. Boy, it was good to see him sweating this out.

"Of course, your families will have to pay for the damages."

"My dad's a builder," Jared said. "You can fix up that house, can't you, Dad?"

"And who do you think is going to pay for that?" Mr. McCain said. His jaw was clenched in anger. "You and Sean are going to be working this debt off for a long time."

"Don't expect to see any more allowance," Mr. Patterson said to Sean.

"I'm afraid that's not all," Sergeant Turrisi went on. "There will be other consequences for these young men, as well."

"You're not going to send us to jail, are you?" Sean said. His voice was shaking.

"Not jail," the sergeant said. "But it is illegal to set bonfires on the beach, so you will definitely be doing many hours of community service."

"Like picking up litter on the freeway?" Jared said, turning up his nose. He practically spit out the words.

"Exactly," Sergeant Turrisi said. "And many other tasks you may not like, either. I'm going to set up a meeting with Ms. Stern, a social worker who will oversee your community service. She'll be available to meet with you and your parents on Monday, that is, if . . . if you gentlemen can spare a few minutes from your tennis schedule."

"Of course," Mr. Patterson said. I felt bad for him. He looked truly disappointed in Sean.

"As for now, I see no reason to continue to ruin these folks' Sunday," Sergeant Turrisi said. Then looking at us and at all the Bermudez family that was gathered there, she said, "You may go. And thank you all for your cooperation."

We got up and left, getting out of there as fast as

we could. Outside the building, we jumped up and down like crazy idiots. Everyone was so relieved and happy, except for Charlie, who still seemed pale and shaken.

"You did the right thing," I said, putting my arms around her and giving her a big hug. "I'm proud of you."

"Yeah. Just wait until the others hear about this," she said. "I wonder what they're going to say."

"That you're a hero?" I suggested.

"No way," she answered.

I had to agree with her there. Charlie had definitely taken the unpopular road, and she was going to have to suffer the consequences of that, whatever they might be.

Eddie came up to us, a huge smile on his handsome face.

"Thank you," he said. "I am so happy you told the truth. And Lily, she will be happy, too."

Then he reached out and gave Charlie a big hug, which set off a complete hug fest. Candido hugged my dad. Charlie hugged Candido. Tyler hugged Eddie. And yes, I hugged Oscar. Not once, not twice, but three times.

It was pretty nice. Actually, it was very nice. Very, very nice.

Which is all I'm going to say about it.

Victory at Last

....

Chapter 16

"If we hustle, we can still make the tournament," my dad said as we pulled out of the Santa Monica City Hall parking lot.

"I thought you canceled our match," Charlie said.

"Well, I tried to. But Anna Kozlov and Marjorie Shin were already on the road up here. So let's just say, I left the door open. Told them due to unforeseen circumstances beyond our control, we might be a few minutes late."

"Dad, I can't play now," I protested. "I'm all pumped up from everything that just happened there in the police station."

"*Pumped up* are two words I like to hear before a tournament," he said.

"We don't have our stuff," Charlie said.

"Already took care of that. GoGo is meeting us there with your clothes and gear."

"But I promised Oscar we would go out and celebrate," I said.

"Already took care of that, too. Candido is dropping Alicia and the boys off at the Sand and Surf."

"You're kidding?!"

My dad actually laughed. "I figured those nice collared shirts shouldn't go to waste."

As we walked into the lobby of the Sand and Surf Club, GoGo was waiting for us with our tennis bags in hand. Right in back of her, the two old guys in their navy blazers were sitting on the red velvet chairs behind the huge mahogany table. Mr. I-Don't-Have-Much-of-a-Mustache was none too pleased to see us. Well, I don't know how he felt about Charlie, but I can tell you this, he was none too pleased to see me.

"Here comes the little tennis player with the big temper," he said. "Do you remember her, Ted?"

The guy named Ted straightened his red striped tie and looked at me over the top of his glasses.

"Yes, indeed," he said. "That was quite a tantrum you threw the last time you were here. We don't approve of tantrums at the Sand and Surf Club."

"Seems like there's a long list of stuff you folks don't approve of," I said. "I know collarless shirts are high on that list."

"We believe in the elegance of traditional country club wear," Mr. Pathetic Mustache said. "Someone has to maintain the dress standards or else who knows what might happen."

"Yeah, next thing you know people are going to run around in red shorts or—heaven forbid—yellow polka-dot skorts," I said, faking horror at the thought. "That will lead us directly down the path to ruin."

"I think you made your point, Doodle," GoGo whispered. "Enough is enough."

Charlie grabbed my arm.

"We don't have time for this, Sams. Let it go. We have to be changed and on the court in less than five minutes."

"You go in the bathroom and get started," I said to her. "I just want to make sure Oscar and Eddie get in okay."

One minute later, they came cruising up in Candido's red truck. The brakes screeched as the truck pulled to a stop in front of the etched glass lobby door. Mustache Man stood up and peered out, casting a disapproving look. Oscar climbed out of the front seat, and Eddie and Alicia slid out of the back. They waved good-bye to Candido and he drove off across the parking lot, attracting quite a bit of attention from the other members. GoGo once told us that the people at Sand and Surf are wound up so tight, they make the Sporty Forty members seem like hippies.

Oscar walked in first and came right up to the two men at the desk. He had his old personality back, bouncy and full of fun.

"We're here to see our friends play," he said. "And we have very big collars on."

"Indeed you do," Ted said to him. "Court thirteen, sir."

Oscar took Alicia's arm and strode across the lobby. He looked so happy and confident that for a moment, I forgot all about his clubfoot. The person I saw was walking tall, proud to be there.

Charlie was already changed when I got to the bathroom. Quickly, I threw on my clothes and got out my racket. There was going to be no time to warm up. We were going to have to face Kozlov and Shin just the way we were.

As we hurried down the path to court thirteen, we bumped into our dad and GoGo.

"I want you to concentrate out there," Dad said, falling in step with us. "Focus. Center down. Don't let anything distract you. Especially you, Charlie."

"Me?" Charlie said. "I always focus. It's Sammie who's the flake."

"Well, there are some special circumstances on the court that might distract you. I'm just saying to ignore them."

The announcer was calling our names over the public address system, so there was no time to ask what special circumstances he was talking about. But as soon as we hurried onto the court, I saw immediately what they were. Lauren Wadsworth was sitting in the front row of the stands, sipping Frappuccinos with

Brooke and Jillian. She didn't look pleased to see us. Actually, she never looks pleased to see me, but she gave Charlie a particularly dark look.

All the color drained from Charlie's face. She looked like someone had punched her in the gut.

"Lauren looks really mad," she whispered to me.

"Don't talk to her now," I said to Charlie. "Remember what Dad said. We have to focus."

We shook hands with Kozlov and Shin, and then went to the bench to put down our gear. Before anyone could stop her, Lauren was out of the stands and courtside, marching right up to Charlie and getting in her face.

"I heard what happened this morning," she said. "Everyone knows."

"We just left the police station a half hour ago," Charlie said. "How do you know?"

"Sean called the General from the bathroom," she said. "The General called Brooke, and she told me."

"It's all hearsay," I said.

"I have no idea what that is, Sammie," Lauren said. "And besides, this is none of your business. My conversation with Charlie is only for SF2 ears."

"You better put some diamond studs in them then," I said.

Okay, maybe not the funniest joke in the world, but I'm pretty pleased with it.

"You double-crossed us," Lauren said to Charlie. "That's not the SF2 way."

"Please don't be mad at me," Charlie begged. "I had to tell what I knew. Otherwise, Oscar wasn't going to get his leg fixed. I couldn't have that on my conscience."

"Who cares about your stupid conscience?" Lauren snapped.

"I do," I snapped back.

"I thought I made it clear this wasn't any of your business," Lauren said, curling her lip at me. The official was motioning to her to get off the court so we could begin the game. But no one tells Lauren Wadsworth what to do.

"I thought you were a friend, Charlie," she went on. "We took you in and made you one of us. We trusted you. And now look what you've done. Sean and Jared are going to have to do stupid community service. And they're not going to have any spending money for at least a hundred years. All to protect your little Mexican friends."

That took my breath away. I looked at Charlie to see what she was going to do. Once again, I hoped and prayed that she would act like the sister I knew, the sister I loved.

And thank goodness, she didn't let me down. Lauren had crossed the line, especially the part about Oscar and Eddie being "our little Mexican friends." I could see Charlie's attitude shift right there in front of me, the minute Lauren said those words. It was like she instantly transformed from a scared kid to a strong, confident grown-up. Just like nerdy little Clark Kent does when he runs into a phone booth and changes into Superman.

"Lauren, that is a terrible thing to say," Charlie said without flinching or batting an eye. "First of all, Oscar and Eddie are not Mexican. They're from El Salvador. And second of all, it doesn't matter where they're from or whether they wear cool clothes or what color their skin is. Oscar was innocent and he didn't deserve to be punished for what Jared and Sean did."

"Well, aren't you Little Miss Perfect," Lauren said. "Since when did you get so goody-goody?"

"You can call it what you want, Lauren. But I know that I've been a good friend to you. And I didn't do what I did to hurt you. I did it to help Oscar. I'd like you to be able to understand that."

"Well, I have news for you," Lauren said. "I don't understand it at all. In fact, after what you did, I don't want to be friends with you. No one does."

She waved to Jillian and Brooke. They came trotting over like the good little followers they were.

"What's up?" Brooke said.

"We're leaving," Lauren answered. "We have better things to do with our time than watch a couple of jock girls play some stupid game."

Just like that, the three girls with the bounciest hair on planet Earth marched off the court without so much as a backward glance.

A Date for a Date

Chapter 17

"I'm nervous to see him," I said to Alicia as we walked into the lobby of Children's Hospital. "I hope he's not in pain."

A week had passed since the match with Kozlov and Shin. Charlie and I played some of the best tennis we've ever played that day. Even Mustache Man and Ted left their post at the mahogany table in the lobby and came to watch our last set. Charlie was fired up by anger at Lauren. I was fired up by love for my courageous sister. It was a powerful combination. Not only did we win, we got written up in the Sand and Surf newsletter as the doubles team to watch in the Under-14 category. They said we even had a chance of making national finals.

They ran pictures of us, too. Charlie looked

great—not all made up like she was for the fund-raiser, but when she was holding our trophy and laughing and glowing with pride, she was a knockout. That was a much better look for her than the top-model game she had been trying to play. As for me, I have to be honest. I didn't look so hot. Well, actually, the problem was that I looked *too* hot. You could actually see sweat dribbling down my upper lip. And as usual, my hair had turned that lovely shade of baby-poop brown. The only thing I needed to be a total embarrassment to the Sand and Surf Club was a yellow polka-dot skort.

When Dr. Mandel learned that Jared and Sean were the ones who set the fire, he called Oscar and told him the surgery was back on. We celebrated the news, and our big tournament win, with pizza and frozen yogurt at Antonio's. We invited everyone in the Bermudez family to come. Eddie invited Lily, who showed up looking her usual fabulous self in a fringed suede jacket, a red bandanna around her neck, and vintage cowboy boots.

"Wow," Oscar said. "You look like our grandfather Eduardo. He lives on a ranch in the mountains and rides horses all day."

"You're crazy, Oscar," Eddie said. "Grandfather Eduardo has a black mustache and a big belly. Lily is beautiful."

"Watch out for my nephew," Candido said, pulling out a chair for Lily to sit down. "He is in love with love."

We ordered pizzas and drinks and delicious

buttery garlic bread. In between the pepperoni chomping, Oscar presented Charlie and me with a drawing he had done.

"This drawing of Iron Man is for you, Charlie," he said, "because you showed me you are strong like iron. And, Sammie, this one is for you."

"Who'd you get?" Charlie asked me.

"Wonder Woman," Oscar answered.

"I get it," Ryan said. "Because Sammie can block bullets with her bracelets."

"No," Oscar said simply. "Because she is cool."

Just as Candido was standing up to make a toast to thank us for coming forward to defend Oscar, Lauren Wadsworth walked into the restaurant with her mom, dad, and little sister.

I watched Charlie carefully. The minute she saw Lauren, she smoothed her hair and tried to smile. Chip Wadsworth came over to our table.

"Terrible about Jared and Sean," he said. "They're going to have to learn their lesson the hard way."

"It's such a shame," Mrs. Wadsworth added. "They're such nice boys."

No one at our table spoke up to agree with her. After an awkward silence, she turned to Lauren and said, "Honey, do you want to invite Charlie and Lily to join us at our table?" Then looking at GoGo, she whispered, "The girls are such great friends, I know they hate to be apart."

Obviously, she hasn't heard the news.

Charlie's eyes lit up at the invitation, but before she could answer, Lauren spoke up.

"That's okay, Mom. I think Charlie should stay right where she is."

"Oh," Mrs. Wadsworth said, looking a little confused. "How about you, Lily? Do you want to come sit with Lauren?"

"No, thanks, Mrs. Wadsworth," Lily answered. "I'm happy where I am, too."

Lauren put her tiny nose in the air and pointed her expensive pink patent leather shoes in the direction of the Wadsworths' table. As she stomped away, I glanced over at Charlie. She looked like someone had hit her in the face. There were the beginnings of tears forming in the corners of her eyes. Maybe no one else could see them, but I could. And GoGo could, too. She reached out and took Charlie's hand.

"False friends come and go," she said. "But true friends are with you forever."

"I know, GoGo," Charlie said. "It just hurts, that's all."

"You can be friends with us," Alicia said. "We're pretty fun, aren't we, Sammie?"

"A laugh a minute," I said.

"And there's always me," Lily said. "I may be in the market for some new best friends. I know I'm no Lauren Wadsworth, but hey, I am what I am."

Charlie half smiled at that. But when Lily turned her attention back to Eddie, I noticed that Charlie grew very quiet. I could see her watching Lauren out of the corner of her eye. I'm sure she was wondering what was going to happen with her and Spencer. And I was also sure she was hoping Lauren would come over and apologize, tell her how wrong she was, and how much she still wanted to be friends.

Of course, Lauren did no such thing. But something pretty sweet happened instead. When we got home after dinner, Charlie came running into the living room where I was watching *The Simpsons* with Ryan, waving her phone around like it was a flag on the Fourth of July.

"Hey, look!" she shouted, pointing at the screen.

"No offense, Charles," Ryan said, "but you're standing in front of the TV. This may come as a shocker, but I can't see through you."

"Read this," she said, pointing to her phone. "It's from Spencer."

"All right," Ryan sighed. "Anything to get you to move over." He looked at her phone and read the text. "'Hey, you. Congrats on a great tennis match today.'" Ryan just stared at Charlie. "And this is the reason you are interrupting one of the greatest animated series ever to be on television?" he asked.

"Read the rest of it," Charlie said.

"No. I'm over this game."

"Okay, Sammie, you read it."

I took the phone and read the rest of the text.

"'I was hoping that you could go with me to

the football game at Santa Monica High next Friday. What do you say? Spencer.' You see?" I squealed. "I told you he was a decent guy. I knew he'd be on your side."

Charlie jumped up and down like a jack-in-the-box and I joined right in. Poor Ryan. He just sat there shaking his head and moaning about how he got sisters instead of brothers. But secretly, I think he was happy for Charlie. I know I was.

I wasn't allowed to go visit Oscar for the first five days after his operation. It was a very complicated surgery involving tendons and bones and other painful-sounding stuff. At first, they put him in a brace and he had to stay really still. But then they took off the brace and put his leg in a cast. That kept everything in just the right position to heal, which meant he was allowed to move around a little and have visitors. He told Alicia that I was the first person he wanted to see. That was all I needed to hear. We got Candido to drop us off at the hospital while he went to the drug store to get supplies Oscar would need when he was ready to come home.

That gave us half an hour alone with Oscar. I

was nervous because I didn't know what to expect. Like the lobby. You'd think the lobby of a children's hospital would be a depressing place. But not this one. It was filled with mosaics of superheroes and colorful planets. There were toys everywhere, and little kids sitting with their parents doing puzzles and reading books. We walked through the lobby and made our way to the elevator. Oscar was on the fourth floor. When the elevator stopped on the third floor, a little boy sitting on a black gurney was wheeled in by a nurse. He was wearing Batman pajamas.

"Hi. This is my Batmobile," he said. "I drive it all over the hospital."

"Do you know a boy named Oscar?" I asked. "He has a big cast on his leg."

"Sure," he said. "He's funny. He has a Batmobile, too."

When we got off the elevator on the fourth floor, he waved good-bye and said to say hi to Oscar. We made our way down the long hall to Oscar's room—407A. I pushed the door open and peeked inside, bracing myself in case Oscar looked really sick or pale or pained. But what I saw was nothing. The bed was empty, and there was no Oscar to be found.

"I'll go to the nurse's station and check on his room number," Alicia said. "Maybe they moved him. You wait here."

She left and I sat down on the edge of the green

plastic chair and waited. There were drawings of superheroes taped to the wall, including a beautiful one of the Human Torch with orange and yellow flames decorating the edges of the paper. Yeah, this had to be Oscar's room. Suddenly, I heard his voice coming down the hall.

"Woo-hoo," he was shouting. "Watch me fly!"

Within seconds, the door to Room 407A burst open and Oscar came rolling in. He was sitting up on a black gurney, just like the one the little boy had, and being pushed by a nurse. Oscar's leg was in a big cast, from the middle of his thigh all the way down to his toes.

"Sammie!" he yelled. "Look, Doug. It's my girlfriend, Sammie. Didn't I tell you she was beautiful?"

Wait a minute. Did he say girlfriend?

The nurse smiled at me. "You picked yourself a real live wire," he said. "Oscar is keeping us all in stitches."

"No, it's me who has stitches," Oscar said.

Doug cracked up. "What'd I tell you?" he said. "Oscar's one great kid. How long have you guys known each other?"

"About two weeks," Oscar said. "I call her *mi corazón.*"

"Well, you did once," I corrected him.

"He's a real Romeo," Doug said to Oscar, giving him that boy-thing playful punch in the arm. "How about if I go get you two lovebirds a snack from the kitchen?"

"Red Jell-O," Oscar said, nodding. "It tastes like strawberries," he said to me.

"Can I get you one, Sammie?" Doug asked.

"Sure. That'd be great. Thank you."

"Don't you move, partner," Doug said to Oscar as he put the brakes on his gurney and checked to make sure his leg was comfortable. "You wait right there until I get back."

"No worries." Oscar laughed. "I'm just going to sit here and look at *mi corazón*." He was really embarrassing me.

When Doug left, I reached into my backpack and brought out a tin with a picture of Iron Man on it. I handed it to him.

"GoGo made you cookies," I said. "She said you should eat them to give you superhealing powers."

He popped the tin open and shoved one of the cookies into his mouth.

"*Delicioso*," he said. "I feel better already."

"I have something else for you." I took out an envelope addressed to him and handed it over. He gave it right back to me.

"You read it to me, Sammie. It's hard for me to read in English."

I opened the envelope and read.

"'Dear Oscar, I am so happy you were able to get your leg fixed after all. Please come visit me in the Governor's Mansion as soon as you recover. All the best to you, Governor Diane Corday.'"

Oscar's eyes nearly popped out of his head.

"She wrote this letter to me? The president of California?"

"She's the governor ... and yes, she wrote it to you and had it dropped off at the beach club."

"But I am just a boy from El Salvador," Oscar said, shaking his head in disbelief. "Why would such an important person write to me?"

"Because you're pretty cool," I said.

"And you are pretty beautiful," he answered.

I didn't know what to say. I'd never had a boy like me before. And I for sure had never had any boy tell me he thought I was beautiful. It felt pretty great, but I wasn't sure what I was supposed to do next. So I got a serious look on my face and said, "Oscar, you have to stop that." But the voice inside me was saying, *oh please, don't stop*!

I thought he was going to fall off his gurney when I handed him the last present I brought. It was a copy of *Los Angeles* magazine, and guess whose picture was on the cover?

I'll give you a hint. It wasn't Lauren Wadsworth's.

The magazine had published a story about Oscar, the kid from San Francisco Gotera who came to America to get his leg fixed. It was called "Oscar Bermudez: A Real Life Superhero."

"That's me!" Oscar whistled. "My face! How did it get there?"

I pointed to the words at the bottom of the cover

and read them aloud. "Story and photos by Tyler Frank."

Oscar took the magazine and put it next to his heart. "I will keep this always," he said. "I will show it to everyone in my town. I have never been so proud of anything."

As he reached down to put the magazine on the table next to his bed, I saw him wince with pain. I realized we hadn't talked at all about the surgery.

"How are you feeling, Oscar?" I asked him.

"It hurts," he said. "But that's okay. It will take a while, but before too long, I will be healed. The doctors say my leg will be almost normal. Do you know what that means, Sammie?"

I shook my head.

"It means that I can throw away that stupid boot. It means I won't limp anymore. It means I will be able to dance with you. Will you dance with me, Sammie?"

"Sure, Oscar. But I have to warn you, I'm a pretty lousy dancer."

"I don't believe that. I think you can do anything you want, just like Wonder Woman."

I couldn't help but smile. This guy had a crush on me, and it felt really nice.

"Let's make a date for our first dance," he said. "One year from today."

"I just so happen to be free one year from today." I smiled. And when he smiled back at me with those gorgeous white teeth and dark, shining eyes, I have to confess my heart did a little happy dance. I had no idea what the next year would bring. Oscar would go home to El Salvador to get better. Maybe he'd come back and visit. I hoped he would. But at that moment, the future didn't matter. All that mattered was the way I felt right then and there.

Happy. Loved. Beautiful. And, yes, even thin.

Or at least, not fat.

There was a knock on the door and Doug came back in.

"Here's your snack," he said. "Knock yourselves out."

So it was that Oscar Bermudez and I sat there in Room 407A, laughing and talking and eating red Jell-O together.

And let me tell you this, my friends. No Jell-O ever tasted so sweet.